Why You'll Love This Book
by Sophie McKenzie

What an amazing book! I mean, *what* an amazing book!

I love *The Kingdom by the Sea* for lots of reasons. For a start, there's the way it begins… grabbing you on page one and never letting go. The story is set in the North East of England during the Second World War. Page one plunges the main character, Harry, into the middle of an air raid. Sirens, noise, confusion and exploding bombs. By the end of the first chapter, Harry has lost everything – his home, his family, even his rabbits. Reading it the first time, I was already completely hooked.

As Harry goes on the run he has to deal with some of life's biggest challenges – finding food and shelter on a daily basis. He finds a purpose – trying to get to the island of Lindisfarne – and someone to care for – Don, the dog. As he travels around, he grows up – and this is another fantastic part of the book; the way without either us or him realising it, Harry changes and learns how to look after himself.

There's a perfect balance in the story between exciting action where Harry faces terrible dangers, and Harry's thoughts and feelings about his situation. You get completely inside Harry's head and the book is really emotional, without ever being sentimental. And that's another thing I love – the beautiful style in which the story is written. Every word counts. Nothing excessive. Nothing wasted.

Harry meets a variety of people on his travels. Some are kind and helpful, others abusive or manipulative. Harry calls himself a pilgrim at one point and, indeed, *The Kingdom by the Sea* is like a quest story, with Harry having to face life-threatening dangers and gain confidence before coming to the end of his journey.

Perhaps my favourite thing about this book is the ending. Don't worry, I'm not going to give it away here! Often when I read stories the endings are disappointing. After a good story, the final pages are predictable or unrealistic. Not with *The Kingdom by the Sea*. As I was reaching the end of the book, I started wondering how it would finish. I was so caught up in Harry's life and adventures I could only see two alternative endings. In the end, the story ended in a third way – one I hadn't foreseen but which felt completely convincing.

This is such a brilliant book – it definitely inspired me to be a better writer and, most importantly, was – and is – one of the best reads, ever!

THE KINGDOM BY THE SEA

Sophie McKenzie

Sophie McKenzie is the award-winning author of *Girl, Missing* and *Six Steps to a Girl*. She was born in London, where she still lives, and worked as a journalist and editor before being able to concentrate on writing full time. In her spare time, Sophie enjoys watching football and going to the movies. Her other books include *Blood Ties* and *The Set-Up*, the first in The Medusa Project series.

For Miriam, who understood

First published in Great Britain by Methuen Children's Books Ltd in 1990
This reissued edition published by HarperCollins *Children's Books* 2009

HarperCollins *Children's Books* is a division of HarperCollins*Publishers* Ltd,
77–85 Fulham Palace Road, Hammersmith, London W6 8JB

The HarperCollins website address is
www.harpercollins.co.uk

1

Copyright © 1990 The Estate of Robert Westall
Why You'll Love This Book copyright © Sophie McKenzie 2009

ISBN-13: 978 000 730141 6

Printed and bound in England by
Clays Ltd, St Ives plc

Mixed Sources
Product group from well-managed
forests and other controlled sources
www.fsc.org Cert no. SW-COC-1806
© 1996 Forest Stewardship Council

FSC is a non-profit international organisation established to promote the
responsible management of the world's forests. Products carrying the FSC
label are independently certified to assure consumers that they come
from forests that are managed to meet the social, economic and
ecological needs of present and future generations.

Find out more about HarperCollins and the environment at
www.harpercollins.co.uk/green

(essentialmodernclassics)

THE KINGDOM BY THE SEA

ROBERT WESTALL

HarperCollins *Children's Books*

Author's Note:

This is a novel: not a geography book. I have taken
a few liberties with my beloved Northumberland:
most with the refuge towers at Lindisfarne.

Chapter One

He was an old hand at air raids now.

As the yell of the siren climbed the sky, he came smoothly out of his dreams. Not scared. Only his stomach clamped down tight for action, as his hands found his clothes laid ready in the dark. Hauled one jumper, then another, over his pyjamas. Thrust both stockinged feet together through his trousers and into his shoes. Then bent to tie his laces thoroughly. A loose lace had tripped him once, in the race to the shelter. He remembered the smashing blow as the ground hit his chin; the painful week after, not able to eat with a bitten tongue.

He grabbed his school raincoat off the door, pulling the

door wide at the same time. All done by feel; no need to put the light on. Lights were dangerous.

He passed Dulcie's door, heard Mam and Dulcie muttering to each other, Dulcie sleepy and cross, Mam sharp and urgent. Then he thundered downstairs, the crack of light from the kitchen door lighting up the edge of each stair-tread. Dad was sitting in his warden's uniform, hauling on his big black boots, his grey hair standing up vertically in a bunch, like a cock's comb. Without looking up, Dad said, "Bloody Hitler! Four bloody nights in a row!"

There was a strong smell of Dad's sweaty feet, and the fag he had burning in the ashtray. That was all Harry had time to notice; he had his own job; the two objects laid ready in the chair by the door. The big roll of blankets, wrapped in a groundsheet because the shelter was damp, done up with a big leather strap of Dad's. And Mam's precious attaché case with the flask of hot coffee and insurance policies and other important things, and the little bottle of brandy for emergencies. He heaved the blankets on to his back, picked up the case with one hand and reached to unlock the back door with the other.

"Mind that light," said Dad automatically. But Harry's hand was already reaching for the switch. He'd done it all a hundred times before.

He slammed the door behind him, held his breath and

listened. A single aircraft's engines, far out to sea. *Vroomah, vroomah, vroomah.* A Jerry. But nothing to worry about yet. Two guns fired, one after another. Two brilliant points of white, lighting up a black landscape of greenhouse, sweet-pea trellises and cucumber-frames. A rolling carpet of echoes. Still out to sea. Safe, then.

He ran down the long back garden, with his neck prickling and the blankets bouncing against his back comfortingly. As he passed the greenhouse the rabbits thumped their heels in alarm. There was a nice cold smell of dew and cabbages. Then he was in through the shelter door, shoving the damp, mould-stinking curtain aside.

He tossed the things on to Mam's bunk, found the tiny oil-lamp on the back girder, and lit it and watched the flame grow. Then he lit the candle under the pottery milk-cooler that kept the shelter warm. Then he undid the bundle and laid out the blankets on the right bunks and turned back to the shelter door, ready to take Dulcie from Mam. He should be hearing their footsteps any second now, the patter of Mam's shoes and the crunch of Dad's hobnailed boots. Dad always saw them safe in the shelter, before he went on duty. Mam would be nagging Dad – had he locked the back door against burglars? They always teased Mam about that; she must think burglars were bloody brave, burgling in the middle of air raids.

God, Mam and Dad were taking their time tonight. What was keeping them? That Jerry was getting closer. More guns were firing now. The garden, every detail of it, the bird-bath and the concrete rabbit, flashed black, white, black, white, black. There was a whispering in the air. Gun-shrapnel falling like rain… they shouldn't be out in *that*. Where were they? Where *were* they? Why weren't they tumbling through the shelter door, panting and laughing to be safe?

That Jerry was right overhead. *Vroomah. Vroomah. Vroomah.*

And then the other whistling. Rising to a scream. Bombs. Harry began to count. If you were still counting at ten, the bombs had missed you.

The last thing he remembered was saying "seven".

His back hurt and his neck hurt. His hands scrabbled, and scrabbled damp clay, that got under his fingernails. The smell told him he was still in the shelter, but lying on the damp floor. And a cautious, fearful voice, with a slight tremble in it, was calling out:

"Is anybody down there?"

Somebody pushed the curtain across the shelter door aside, and shone a torch on him. The person was wearing a warden's helmet, the white 'W' glimmering in the light of the torch. He thought at first it might be Dad. But it wasn't Dad. It had a big black moustache; it was a total stranger.

The stranger said, to somebody else behind him, "There's only one of them. A kid."

"Jesus Christ," said the somebody else. "Ask him where the rest are. There should be four in this shelter."

"Where's the rest, son? Where's your mam and dad?"

"In the… I don't know."

"D'you mean, still in the house, son?"

The voice behind muttered, "Christ, I hate this job." Then it said, with a sharp squeak of fear, "What's that?"

"What's *what*?"

"Something soft under me foot. Shine your light."

"'Sonly a rabbit. A dead rabbit."

"Thank God. Hey, son, can you hear me? Can you get up? Are you hurt?"

Why didn't the man come down and help him? What was he so *frightened* of?

Harry got up slowly. He hurt nearly all over, but not so badly that he couldn't move. The man gave him a hand and pulled him up out of the shelter. Harry peered up the garden. He could see quite well because the sky to the west was glowing pink.

There was no greenhouse left.

There was no house left. The houses to each side were still standing, though their windows had gone, and their slates were off.

"Where's our house?"

There was a silence. Then the man with the moustache said, "What's yer name, son?" Harry told him.

"And what was yer dad's name? And yer mam's?" He wrote it all down in a notebook, like the police did, when they caught you scrumping apples.

He gave them Dulcie's name too. He tried to be helpful. Then he said, "Where *are* they?" and began to run up the garden path.

The man grabbed him, quick and rough.

"You can't go up there, son. There's a gas leak. A bad gas leak. Pipe's fractured. It's dangerous. It's against the law to go up there."

"But my mam and dad're up there…"

"Nobody up there now, son. Come down to the Rest Centre. They'll tell you all about it at the Rest Centre."

Harry just let himself be led off across some more gardens. It was easy, because all the fences were blown flat. They went up the path of number five. The white faces of the Humphreys, who lived at number five, peered palely from the door of their shelter. They let him pass, without saying anything to him.

In the road, the wardens who were leading him met two other wardens.

"Any luck at number nine?"

"Just this lad…"

There was a long, long silence. Then one of the other wardens said, "We found the family from number seven. They were in the garden. The bomb caught them as they were running for the shelter…"

"They all right?"

"Broken arms and legs, I think. But they'll live. Got them away in the ambulance."

Harry frowned. The Simpsons lived at number seven. There was some fact he should be able to remember about the Simpsons. But he couldn't. It was all… mixed up.

"Come on, son. Rest Centre for you. Can you walk that far?"

Harry walked. He felt like screaming at them. Only that wouldn't be a very British thing to do. But something kept building up inside him; like the pressure in his model steam-engine.

Where *was* his steam-engine?

Where was Mam, who could cuddle him and make everything all right?

Where was Dad in his warden's uniform, who would sort everything out?

Next second, he had broken from their hands, and was running up another garden path like a terrified rabbit. He went through another gate, over the top of another air-raid shelter, through a hedge that scratched him horribly… on, and on, and on.

He heard their voices calling him as he crouched in hiding. They seemed to call a long time. Then one of them said, "That wasn't very clever."

"It's the shock. Shock takes them funny ways. You can never tell how shock's going to take them."

"Hope he's not seriously hurt, poor little bleeder."

'Kid that can run like that…?"

And then their voices went away, leaving him alone.

So he came to his house, slowly, up his garden.

He found his three rabbits; they were all dead, though there wasn't a mark on them. Where the greenhouse had been was a tangle of wrecked tomato plants, that bled green, and gave off an overpowering smell of tomato.

The house was just a pile of bricks. Not a very high pile, because everything had fallen down into the old cellar.

There was a smell of gas; but the gas was burning. Seeping up through the bricks and burning in little blue points of flame, all in the cracks between the bricks. It looked like a burning slag-heap, and he knew why the wardens had given up hope and gone away.

He knew he must go away too. Before anybody else found him, began to ask him questions, and do things to him. Because he felt like a bomb himself, and if anyone did anything to him, he would explode into a million pieces and nobody would ever be able to put him back together again.

Especially, he mustn't be given to Cousin Elsie. Cousin Elsie, who would clutch his head to her enormous bosom, and sob and call him "poor bairn" and tell everybody who came all about it, over and over and over again. He'd seen her do that when Cousin Tommy died of diphtheria. Cousin Elsie was more awful than death itself.

No, he would go away. Where nobody knew him. Where nobody would make a fuss. Just quietly go away.

Having made his mind up, he felt able to keep moving. There were useful things to do. The blankets in the shelter to bundle up and take with him. The attaché case. All proper, as Mam and Dad would have wanted it.

It seemed to take him a long time to get the blankets bundled up exactly right and as he wanted them.

In the faint light before dawn, he even managed to find Dad's spade and bury his three rabbits. They had been his friends; he didn't want anybody finding them and making a meal of them. He even found some wooden seed markers, and wrote the rabbits' names on them, and stuck them in for tombstones.

Then he went, cutting across the long stretch of gardens and out into Brimble Road, where hardly anybody knew him.

He looked dirty, tear-stained, and exactly like a refugee. His face was so still and empty, nobody, even Cousin Elsie, would have recognised him.

He felt… he felt like a bird flying very high, far from the world and getting further away all the time. Like those gulls who soar on summer thermals and then find they cannot get down to earth again, but must wait till the sun sets, and the land cools, and the terrible strength of the upward thermal releases them to land exhausted. Only he could not imagine *ever* coming to earth again, ever. Back to where everything was just as it always had been, and you did things without thinking about them.

He supposed he would just walk till he died. It seemed the most sensible thing to do.

Chapter Two

He must have wandered round the town all day, in circles. Every so often, he would come to himself, and realise he was in Rudyerd Street, or Nile Street.

But what did Rudyerd Street *mean*? What did Nile Street *mean*? Sometimes he thought he would go home, and Dulcie would be swinging on the front gate, shouting rude things at the big boys as they passed, but running to the safety of Mam's kitchen if they made a move to attack her. And Mam would be doing the ironing, or putting the stew in the oven.

But the moment he turned his steps towards home, the truth came back to him; the burning pile of bricks. And he would turn his steps away again.

The last time he came to himself, he was somewhere quite different.

On the beach. The little beach inside the harbour mouth, that didn't have to be fenced off with barbed wire because it was under the direct protection of the Castle guns.

He suddenly felt very tired and sat down with a thump on the sand, with his back against a black tarry boat. He closed his eyes and laid back his head; the warmth of the sun smoothed out his face, like Mam had often done with her hands. He smelt the tar of the boat and it was a nice smell; it was the first thing he'd smelt since the burning gas, and it was a comforting smell. The sun warmed his hands as they lay on the sand, and his knees under his trousers, and in a very tiny world, it was nice, nice, nice. It felt as if somebody *cared* about him, and was looking after him.

On the edge of sleep, he said, "Mam?" questioningly. And then he was asleep.

He dreamed it was just a usual day at home, with Dulcie nagging on, and Mam baking, and Dad coming in from work and taking his boots off with a satisfied sigh. He dreamed he shouted at them, "*There* you all are! Where have you *been*?"

And they all laughed at him, and said, "Hiding, silly!" And it was all right.

The all-rightness stayed with him when he woke; a

feeling they were not far away. He lay relaxed; as he remembered lying relaxed in his pram when he was little and watching the leaves of trees blowing, whispering and sunlit overhead. As long as he didn't move he knew the bubble of happiness would not break. But if he moved, he knew they would go away and leave him again.

So he lay on, dreamily. The sun still shone, though it was setting, and the shadows of the cliff were creeping out towards him. And that he knew was bad. When the shadow reached him the sun would be gone, the world would turn grey, a cold breeze would blow.

And it would be time to go home. Like the three girl bathers who were walking up the beach towards him, chattering and laughing and feebly hitting each other with wet towels. They had a home; he had no home. There was a sort of glass wall between people who had a home and people who hadn't.

He watched them pass and get into a little black car that was waiting to pick them up. He thought, with a twinge of resentment, that *some* people could still get petrol for cars even in wartime. Black market. It would serve them right if the police caught them.

Then the car moved off with a puff of blue smoke, and he felt even more lonely. The shadow of the cliff grew nearer. And nearer.

"Please help," he said to the soft warm air, and the dimming blue sky. "Don't leave me." He felt the approach of another night alone as if it was a monster.

The shadow of the cliff was only a yard away now. He reached out his arm and put his hand into it; it felt cold, like putting your hand in water, icy water.

And yet still he hoped, as the shadow crept up his arm.

He closed his eyes and felt the shadow creeping, like the liquid in a thermometer. Only it wasn't recording heat, it was recording cold.

And then he heard an explosive snort, just in front of him. Sat upright, startled, and opened his eyes.

It was a dog. A dog sitting watching him. A dog who had been in the sea, because its black fur was all spikes. A dog who had been rolling in the sand, because the spikes were all sandy. The dog watched him with what seemed to be very kind eyes. But then most dogs had kind eyes.

The dog held its paw up to him, and hesitantly he took it. The dog woofed twice, softly, approvingly, then took its paw back.

Was this his miracle? He looked round swiftly, for an owner, before he let himself hope.

There was no one else on the beach, just him and the dog.

But lots of dogs came down to the beach on their own

and made friends with anybody, for an afternoon. And there was a medal on the dog's collar.

Not breathing, not daring to hope, he pulled the dog to him by the collar, and read the medal.

The dog was called Don, and lived at 12 Aldergrove Terrace.

Harry shut his eyes, and he couldn't even have told himself whether he closed them in gladness or horror.

Aldergrove Terrace had been a very posh and very short terrace. Three weeks ago, Aldergrove Terrace had been hit by a full stick of German bombs. Anybody in Aldergrove who was still alive was in hospital... permanently.

He opened his eyes, and looked at his fellow survivor. The dog was a sort of small, short-legged Alsatian. It looked quite fit, but rather thin and uncared-for. It certainly hadn't been combed in a long time, and people had combed their dogs in Aldergrove every day. It had been that sort of place.

He pulled the dog towards him again, almost roughly. It willingly collapsed against his leg and lay staring out to sea, its mouth open and its tongue gently out. He stroked it. The sandy fur was nearly dry, and he could feel the warmth of its body seeping out damply against his leg.

They stayed that way a long time, a long contented time, just being together. Long ago, they'd had a dog at number nine, but it had got old and died. It was good to have a dog again, and the way the dog delighted in his hand, he knew it was glad to have found somebody as well. He dreamily watched the little waves breaking on the sand; glad he wasn't alone any more.

And then the dog stood up, and shook itself, and whined, watching him with those warm eyes. It wanted something from him.

"What is it, boy?" The sound of his own voice startled him. He hadn't spoken to anybody since he ran away from the wardens. "What do you want, boy?"

The dog whined again, and then nudged with its long nose at the bundle of blankets, sniffing. Then it turned, and nosed at the attaché case, pushing it through the sand.

The dog was hungry. And he had nothing to give it, nothing in the world. And suddenly he felt terribly hungry himself.

It threw him into a panic of helplessness. It was getting dark as well, and he had nothing to eat and nowhere to sleep. He put his face in his hands, and rocked with misery. And then he remembered his father's voice saying, angrily, "Don't flap around like a wet hen. Think, son, *think*."

It was the boat he noticed first; the boat he had been leaning against. The owner had turned it upside-down, to stop the rain getting in, like they always did. But that had been a long time ago. This boat hadn't been used for years;

the black, tarry paint was splitting, peeling, blistering. There was a half-inch crack, where the stern met the side. That meant…

Safety. A hiding place. A roof for the night, if it started to rain. There was a gap on this side, between the boat and the sand. Only six inches, but he could make it bigger. He began to scrabble at the sand with his hands. The sand came easily; it was soft and dry. Soon he managed to wriggle through the hole he had made. Inside, it was dark, apart from the cracks in the stern, where some light came in. But it smelt sweetly of the sea and old tar, and dry wood. The dog wriggled through to join him, licking his face, sure it was a game. He pushed it away and reached out and dragged in the bundle of blankets and the attaché case. There was plenty of room; it was a big boat, a fishing boat. He squatted by the entrance, like an Indian in his wigwam. He'd solved one problem, and it gave him strength.

Now, food. He racked his brains. Then remembered there had always been a big fish and chip shop in Front Street. It wouldn't sell much fish now, because the trawlers were away on convoy-escort. But it still sold chips and sausages cooked in batter. All the fish and chip shops did.

But… money.

He searched desperately through his pockets for odd pennies and ha'pennies.

And his fingers closed on the milled edge of a big fat two-shilling piece. Yesterday had been Thursday, and Dad had given him his week's pocket-money as usual. It all seemed so very far away, but there was the big fat florin in his hand. He rubbed the edge in the dim light, to make sure it was real, not just a penny.

He took a deep breath, and wormed out through the hole again, followed by the dog. He was in a hurry now; his stomach was sort of dissolving into juice at the thought of the battered sausages. He didn't like the idea of leaving his blankets and the precious attaché case behind, but he couldn't carry them and the chips as well. Besides, they would make him look conspicuous. They would have to take their chance, as Dad always said, when he and Harry planted out tiny seedlings, watered them, and left them for the night. Harry shook his head savagely, to shake away the memory, and the sting of hot tears that pricked at his eyes suddenly. He smoothed back the sand to conceal the hole he had dug, and set off for Front Street, the dog running ahead and marking the lamp-posts as if this was an ordinary evening stroll along the sea front.

Even a hundred yards away, the breeze carried the appetising smell to his nostrils. The shop wasn't shut then; he felt full of triumph. There was a crowd of people in the shop and they hadn't drawn the blackout curtains yet.

He pushed open the door, and the dog nosed past him eagerly, nostrils working. The owner of the shop, a tall bald man in a long greasy white apron, looked over the heads of his customers and saw them, and Harry instantly knew he was a very nasty man indeed, even before he opened his mouth.

"Get that dirty great animal out of here! This is a clean shop, a food shop!"

Covered with confusion, blushing furiously, Harry grabbed the dog's collar, and dragged him out. He pushed the dog's bottom to the pavement, and shouted, "Sit! Sit!" The dog looked at him trustingly, wagging his tail, and Harry dived back into the shop again, before the dog changed his mind. He joined the back of the queue which was about six people long.

"Filthy great beast," said the man, to no one in particular. "I don't know what this town's coming to." He shovelled great mounds of golden chips into newspaper and said to the woman helping him, "More batter, Ada," equally nastily.

Harry heard the shop door open again, and the next second, Don was beside him, leaping up at the glass counter with eager paws, and leaving dirty scratchmarks on the glass.

"I told you, get that bloody animal out of here! I won't tell you again!"

Harry grabbed Don a second time. He could feel tears starting to gather in his eyes. He hauled him out, as two more people passed him to join the queue inside. He had lost his place in the queue. And every time somebody else came, Don would come in with them, and he'd always lose his place in the queue, and *never* get served.

He looked round desperately. There was a lamp-post, with two sandbags attached, for use against incendiary bombs. They were tied to the lamp-post with thick string… Harry hauled Don over, undid the string, and slipped it through Don's collar, tied a knot, and fled back into the shop.

"Messing with our sandbags now?" said the man savagely. He seemed to have eyes everywhere but on his own business. "Don't live round here, do you?"

Harry's heart sank. Not living round here was important; he mightn't get served at all now. Shopkeepers looked after their own, these days of rationing.

"And it's a while since your face saw soap an' water. Or yer hair a comb. Where yer from? The Ridges?"

The Ridges was the slummiest council estate in the whole town; it was a downright insult, to anyone who came from the Balkwell.

"No. From the Balkwell," he said stoutly.

"Well, you get back to the Balkwell chip shop, sonny

Jim. We've only enough chips for Tynemouth people in this shop. An' take that damned dog with you. Stolen him, have you? He looks a bit too grand for the likes of you. I've a mind to phone for the poliss."

The tears were streaming down Harry's face by that time. One of the women in the queue said, "Steady on, Jim. The bairn's upset. What's the matter, son?"

Something gave way inside Harry. It was all too much. He said, "I've been bombed out."

He heard a murmur of sympathy from the assembled customers, so he added, "Me dad was killed." He said it like he was hitting the man with a big hammer.

There was a terrible hush in the shop. Everyone was looking at him, pale and open-mouthed. Then the woman said, "Serve him first, Jim. He can have my turn. What do you want, son?"

Harry had only meant to have one portion, to share with the dog. But the wild triumph was too sweet. The dog would have his own; and they'd have one each for breakfast in the morning, too. And he was thirsty.

"Four sausage and chips. And a bottle of Tizer."

Viciously, the man scooped up the portions. Harry thought he tried to make them mingy portions, but all the customers were watching him. So he suddenly doubled-up the number of chips, far more than he should have given.

Then he banged the big newspaper parcel on the counter, and the bottle of Tizer with it.

"Two shillings and fourpence!"

Harry gazed in horror at the two-shilling piece in his hand.

He'd over-reached himself with a vengeance, and he hadn't another penny on him. He stared around panic-stricken at the staring faces.

Then the woman took his two shillings off him, added fourpence of her own, and gave it to the man, saying, "Run along, son. Yer mam could do with those chips while they're hot."

"Ta," he said, staring at her plump kindly face in wonder. Then he was out of the shop, with the burning packet of chips against his chest and the Tizer bottle on the pavement as he untied Don.

He walked back to the boat in a whirl. So much had happened so quickly. But he'd gone to get chips, and he'd done it. Made a terrible mess of mistakes, but he'd *done* it.

He spread the dog's share on the sand, on its newspaper, so the dog wouldn't eat any sand by mistake. The dog wolfed the sausage first, then all the chips, and nosed the folds of paper for every last crumb of batter. Then came to scrounge off Harry. It must have been really starving. Well, now it was full, and he himself had seen to that. He felt obscurely proud. The dog was his, and he'd fed it. And found it a place to sleep.

He stretched his legs out and lay against the boat, relaxed, and swigged Tizer. He couldn't give the dog any Tizer. He hadn't a bowl. But the dog loped off to where a little freshwater stream trickled down the sand from the Castle cliff and lapped noisily. Another problem solved.

He watched the little waves coming in to the beach from the darkening river. Little lines of whiteness coming out of the dark. This time last night they'd all been sitting down to supper, Mam, Dad, Dulcie...

He let himself cry then. Somehow he could afford to, with his belly full, and his new home against his back, and his new friend the dog snuffling at his raincoat, still looking for crumbs of batter. He cried quite a long time, but he cried very quietly, not wanting anyone to hear him, in case they came across to find out what was the matter. The dog licked his tears with a huge wet tongue, and he hugged it to him.

And yet, even as he was crying, he was thinking. Hard. So many things going round in his mind, like a squirrel in a cage.

He must keep himself clean and tidy somehow. A dirty face got you into trouble. He must comb his hair. He must keep his shoes polished and his raincoat clean. And he must get a leash for Don. And he must stay near fresh water to drink… And …

He reached for Don's collar in the dark, twisted off the medal and threw it as far down the beach as he could. That medal was Don's death-sentence. The police caught dogs who'd lost their owners in air raids, and had them put down on an electrified plate at the police station. They dampened the dog's coat, then they electrocuted it. That was what Dad had said had happened to their old dog, when he got too old. He said they did it to some lovely dogs, it was a shame.

Don was his dog now.

As the last tinge of light faded, far out over the sea, he dug under the boat again, crawled in and called the dog in after him. It wouldn't do to be on the beach after dark. People might ask questions.

He spread the blankets neatly, wishing he had a candle to see by. That was something else he'd have to lay his hands on.

He had the sand-hole neatly filled in again when his need to pee caught him in the groin like a knife. Swearing to himself, he dug the hole again, and got outside only just in time. He crawled back, thinking he had an awful lot to learn. He'd always had Mam until now, saying do this, do that, till you could *scream*. Now he had to say do this, do that, to himself.

Still, he was snug. He had enough blankets to make two

into a pillow and give one to the dog. Except the dog snuggled up close to him, and he let it in.

He gave one deep sigh, and was asleep. All night his breathing lay hidden under the greater breathing of the sea. He wakened once, to hear rain patting on the boat. But it only made things cosier.

Chapter Three

The dog wakened him, by licking his face. He had no idea what time it was, but all along the gap between the boat and the sand, the sun was shining. The dog dug its way out with great enthusiasm, showering him with sand, bringing him fully awake. He scrambled out after it.

It was a glorious morning. The sky was blue from horizon to horizon. Little wavelets crept up the beach, gentle as a kiss. The air was still cool, the sun had just risen over the sea, and there wasn't a soul in sight.

His first thought was that he must get clean. He stripped to his underpants, shivering, and walked out into the wavelets. He remembered learning at school that you could get yourself clean with sand, and picked up a handful of liquid sand and scrubbed his hands. He did it three times, and it worked. All the grime vanished, leaving his hands pale and wrinkled with the cold. He got another handful and scrubbed his face. The sand stung, but in a pleasant way. His mouth filled with a salty taste, but that was all right. He remembered also from school that you could clean your teeth with salt; and he cleaned them with a bit of sand and his finger, and spat out. Then he scrubbed himself with sand all over. He felt great, really alive. He wanted to swim, but he didn't want to get his underpants soaking. Then he thought that the sun would dry them, as it had once dried his swimming-costume, and plunged in regardless. The sea was much warmer than the air. He swam and swam. He loved swimming. He imagined he was a fish, without a care in the world.

Then he looked up, and saw the dog's face swimming in front of him. The dog also looked terribly happy, and was carrying a crooked black stick in his mouth. It dropped it in the water in front of him. It wanted it thrown. He tried to stand up in the water, found he was too far out when his head went under, and scrambled back to the shore in a flurry of arms and legs and foam. But he wasn't really worried. This was the Haven, and his dad had always said that the Haven was safe, no undertow, no currents. Safest place in Northumberland.

When he found his footing, the dog brought him the stick again, and he spent ages throwing it out to sea. He thought the dog would never tire but, eventually, it ran up the beach, dived under the boat, and emerged with a newspaper packet in its mouth. Last night's spare sausage and chips…

He yelled at it, suddenly furious. *He* was in charge; the dog was getting above itself. He tried to grab the packet from its mouth, but it wouldn't let go, shaking its head to throw off his hand, and backing away all the time. Beside himself with rage, he hit it with the crooked black stick that he still held in his other hand. It closed its eyes, but it wouldn't let go. He hit it harder, and it growled deep in its throat.

Perhaps it was lucky that the stick broke. He put both hands to the packet of newspaper and pulled with all his might. The newspaper tore on the dog's teeth, and he had it. The dog made a snatch for it, but he held it high in the air.

The dog leapt and knocked him flat. But he kept hold of the packet, clutching it into his armpit as he fell, like a rugby ball at school. The dog kept nosing in, but he twisted and turned. Several times, he felt the dog's naked teeth touch his skin; but the dog didn't bite him.

At last they stopped, and glared at each other. He

couldn't read the look on the dog's face, but he wasn't scared of dogs. He would show it who was boss.

"Sit, boy, sit!"

It sat, at last, tail swishing vigorously. He began to unwrap the packet and it dived in again. He hit it on the nose, and it backed off.

The battle seemed to go on forever, but at last the dog learned to sit still, until he had unwrapped the whole packet and laid out its share. Then it dived in, without waiting for the word of command.

He sat back with a sigh, and ate his own. It was a victory of sorts. He ate his sausage, which tasted good. He thought the chips would be awful, but they tasted good as well. When he was finished he looked down at his bare stomach. It was bulging – but it felt good and solid and cheering. And his underpants, though sandy, were nearly dry. And now the sun touched warmly on his back, and he came out in goose-pimples.

He looked all round, cautiously. There was still nobody about, though there was smoke coming from the chimney of one of the coastguard cottages on the headland. He thought he had time for a quick explore, along the tide-line, where you always found the interesting things.

The dog thought that was great. It began pouncing on all the patches of seaweed, killing them with its feet, dive-bombing them, then throwing them high in the air. He tried calling it to heel, as he had seen men do when they were walking their dogs on the beach.

It ignored him. He made up his mind to work on it. Its disobedience could get them both into trouble. It was then that he found the lump of soaking rope. He tried it for strength, stamping on one end, and pulling the other end with both hands. It seemed pretty strong, and it was one yard long, with frayed ends. He knew there was no point in calling the dog, but he waved the rope enticingly, and the dog came, and he grabbed its collar, and slipped the rope through. The dog promptly took off along the beach, dragging him after it. It was stronger than he was, and heavier. All he could do was hang on. The dog made terrible noises, like it was choking itself to death. But he hung on. He had to win. For both their sakes. It was a good dog, but only young. It had to learn.

Finally, it got tired of strangling itself, and walked quietly by his side. It was then he found the other useful thing. A washing-day ladle, like Mam used. About eight inches across, rusty, but it had no holes in it. It would do to give the dog water in. He came back to the boat full of triumph, and got dressed. As he did, two more pennies fell out of his trouser pocket. He searched every pocket after that, and ended up with threepence ha'penny.

He stared at it, lying in the pale palm of his hand, and despair fell on him, without warning, out of a clear blue sky, like a collapsing house. What good was threepence ha'penny? It wouldn't even buy them a meal to share tonight. Only chips. And when the chips were gone, what then? And the next day, and the next, getting hungrier and hungrier. He could only get food by going to Cousin Elsie's; and he knew what Uncle George would do with the dog. Straight down to the police station.

He stared at the sand for a long, long time. The dog, puzzled, impatient, leapt up and put its paws on his shoulders and looked at him trustingly. He could have died of agony.

And then he remembered his father's voice again.

"Don't flap around like a wet hen. *Think!*"

And immediately, he realised he did have some money. In the Trustee Savings Bank. Seventeen pounds, ten shillings. All the money from all the birthdays and Christmases that Mam had made him save when he wanted to go out and spend it. Saving up for a rainy day, she had called it, when he raged and pleaded with her.

But where was the bank book?

In the attaché case, of course.

He dived in under the boat, and clicked open the case with trembling hands. There was a bundle of bank books, held together neatly by an elastic band. Dad's on top, then Mam's, then his. He opened it. It said, in neat curling writing, seventeen pounds, ten shillings. And he knew how to get it out; you only had to fill in a form, that was all. He had enough to keep himself and the dog for months. Wild excitement blew through him like a gale. He must get it! Now!

Then his eye drifted round the rest of the case; over the other precious things it contained. Dad's best wristwatch, the one he only used for special occasions, in case it got scratched. The bright pink insurance books. A wedding photograph in a small silver frame, with Mam and Dad looking smooth, smiling and young. His own photograph in school uniform, from when he first went to the grammar school; a neat bundle of school reports. How proud of him they'd been! Tears pricked again, so he rushed on, being practical. The family ration books… a bar of Mam's pongy special toilet soap, still in its paper wrapper. The scent wafted up to his nostrils… and he felt suddenly terribly guilty, as if he was burgling a church. He was never allowed to look inside the attaché case; it was private to Mam and Dad.

He took his own bank book and then slammed the case shut and clicked in the fasteners loudly. Well, as long as he carried the attaché case, Mam and Dad would still be with him. Like the Ark of the Covenant that the children of Israel carried all the way to the Promised Land.

To soothe himself, he carefully folded the blankets into a neat heap, then came out of the boat and smoothed down the sand to hide the entrance, and sat playing with the dog's ears till his breathing came back to normal.

Not a moment too soon. There was a man coming out of the coastguard cottage, the one with the smoking chimney. Walking down the beach towards him. Harry could tell from the way he walked that he wasn't a bad bloke. He walked slow and steady and contented, puffing on his pipe, stopping to look at things and touch them. Only a bit bossy, perhaps. As if it was *his* place.

"Good morning, young feller-me-lad! You're the early bird that catches the worm!"

"Been swimming," said Harry.

"So Aah noticed, while Aah was shaving. Said to the missus there was a young feller-me-lad, having a grand time wi' his dog, on a Saturday morning early. Grand dog!" He bent and patted it. "What's his name?"

"Don."

The man looked for a name-medal on the collar and didn't find any. "Dog could do with a combing. Sand won't do his coat no good."

"I always comb him when I get home." Harry was amazed how neatly the lie popped out. Then he said, "What time is it, mister?"

"Half-past eight," said the man, pulling out a pocket watch. "Better be on me way up yonder." He pointed to the Coastguard Station on the cliff. "Just thought Aah'd have a word wi' you, seeing you was having so much fun wi' your dog. Only," he added, "you could do wi' a pair of bathing-trunks, instead of bathing in yer underpants. We'll have young girls down here, later on." He glanced around. "A towel wouldn't do you any harm, either." Harry glanced at him, suddenly hunched-up, wary. But the man gave him a conspiratorial grim. "Aah didn't tell me mam all Aah was doing when Aah was young either." And he was gone, leaving only a fragrant whiff of his tobacco smoke.

Chapter Four

Three hours later, Harry lay back on the sand by the boat, closed his eyes, and let his mind stop whirling. What a terrible trip! He was never, never, never going up into the town again. Tommy Dodds had seen him, and Audrey Henry's mother, and he'd only missed running into Cousin Elsie by diving up a back alley like a shot rabbit. He still wasn't sure she *hadn't* seen him. And the terrible wait in the bank, while the man counted out his money three times before he gave it to him, and he worried about Don tied to a lamp-post outside… when he'd got out, he took the bus straight back to Tynemouth. Thank God he'd had that threepence ha'penny, or he'd have had to give the conductor a ten-shilling note for the fare. And the conductor had still fussed about how sandy the dog was, and how it was making a mess of his bus… It had been stupid to go up into the town on a Saturday when everybody was out shopping. If he went on making stupid mistakes like that, he'd get caught for certain.

But Tynemouth village had been better. Nobody knew him in Tynemouth. And he'd had a good shopping-spree, ten-shilling notes or no ten-shilling notes. There were still things to buy that were not on the rations. The pet-shop woman had been nice and friendly. Sold him a leash for the dog, and a steel curry-comb, and a big bag of dog biscuits. And some anti-flea soap, that would do for them both. She had pursed her lips over the note, but he'd said, "It's me birthday present," and she had told him he was a kind boy, spending all his birthday present on his dog. Then he'd gone to the butcher's, and got some bones for the dog, and looked at the Cornish pasties so hungrily that the man had said, with a grin, "Do you want one? You can't live on doggy-bones, a growing lad like you."

And lastly he had gone to the newsagents, and bought two boxes of matches, because he thought they were sure to come in useful, and the biggest newspaper he could see. Not that he cared a damn about the news, but certain movements in his tummy told him he was going to need a newspaper tonight after dark. God, life was all food going in one end, and out the other.

But for the moment, he was content. Full of Cornish pasty, watching the dog chew at his big bone, and watching the girls go past in their bathing costumes.

Through the pair of dark glasses he'd thought on to buy at the chemist's.

The chip-shop man saw him coming. Long before he got to the shop, Harry could see the bald head peering and bobbing maliciously above the heads of the customers. He had spent half of the day manufacturing lies for the chip-shop man. He tied up Don properly by his leash to the lamp-post, and pushed boldly into the shop.

"Ha," said the man nastily. "Here's our little war hero, back for his nightly share of *our* fish and chips. I see you've managed to wash your face for once."

Harry joined the queue quietly, saying nothing. All the people in the shop were total strangers, so he knew he couldn't look for any help there.

"'E's bombed out, you know," said the man nastily. "Where you billeted then?"

Harry was ready. "Priory Road." It was the longest road in Tynemouth, and not very posh.

"What number?" asked the man. Harry was ready for that, too.

"Dunno," he said, "but it's about half-way down, on the

right-hand side. Gotta green door and big white sea shells in the garden." Half the houses in Priory Road had big white sea shells in the garden.

"What's the lady's name – that you're billeted on?"

"It's a funny long name – we just have to call her Auntie."

There was a titter in the queue. Harry felt they were turning on to *his* side. The woman at the front of the queue said sharply, "C'mon, Jim. I haven't got all night to stand here, you know. Our Ted's got to go back from leave."

The man gave Harry another nasty glare, but started shovelling chips again. Meanwhile, the other women in the queue began discussing which woman with a funny long name had a house in Priory Road, with a green door and sea shells in the front garden.

"It's not Peggy Molyneaux, is it? I hadn't heard she had anybody billeted on her…"

Harry was glad he'd picked the longest road in Tynemouth. But he knew with dreadful certainty that this was the last time he could use the chip shop. The gossip would be all over the village by tomorrow night. And what would he and Don do for food then? The woman asked him more questions about his landlady, and he almost ran out of answers, and sweated.

But at last it was his turn.

"Six sausage an' chips, please." He might as well grab what food he could.

"Six?" yelled the man. "Are ye feeding a bloody regiment or something?"

"The landlady wants some an' all. An' for her husband." Harry's lips quivered. He felt a traitorous tear gathering in his eye, and simply let himself cry. It had worked last night...

"Leave the poor bairn alone, for God's sake," said a woman. "What's he ever done to you, Jim?" And there was a murmur from the queue. Harry didn't think anybody liked the man, really.

But it was a marvellous relief to get out into the cool air of Front Street, with the packet burning against his chest. His tears dried up instantly, and he untied Don and walked down to the sea amazed at himself. His dad had always taught him never to lie, and that only *babies* cried. But tears and lies seemed to be all that worked now.

In the night, the dog stirred against his side. Stirred and growled deep in its throat. Harry was awake in a flash. Was there someone prowling the dark beach? Somebody after Mam's precious attaché case? He listened hard, and heard nothing. Then the dog growled again.

And Harry heard.

Vroomah, vroomah, vroomah. Out over the sea. The Jerry bombers were back. And there seemed to be a lot of them.

Then, on the Castle cliffs overhead, the siren went.

The dog whimpered, once, and then went mad, trying to scrabble its way out from under the boat, casting huge sheets of sand over the blankets, and into Harry's eyes in the dark. His eyes were agony.

But he knew he must stop the dog. Dogs went crazy in air raids. Ran about the streets howling, upsetting people. Ran blind, ran anywhere. Don could run off and get lost forever.

He grabbed for Don's collar, and felt around desperately for the leash, and got it on him, just as the dog wriggled out from under the boat. Harry let himself be dragged after him, bumping his head so he saw stars. There was nothing else he could do.

Outside, it was as light as day. Three searchlights, three great bars of blue light reached outwards from the Castle into the sky above the sea, slowly waving and feeling like fingers for the approaching Jerries. More searchlights waved around from South Shields across the river. Little bits of mist or cloud drifted through the beams, like cigarette smoke. By their light, Harry could see every detail of the beach. And be seen. There'd be a warden round in a minute, yelling at him to get under cover. And the bombers were closer, and the guns would be opening fire overhead. Where to run to?

But the dog just ran, and Harry had to run with him, tripping over bits of wood half-buried in the sand and once falling flat and being dragged along. He hadn't a clue where he was going. But Don had. Suddenly they were up against the beginning of the pier, the massive granite pier. And set into the pier, huge arches. And inside the arches, massive granite blocks were stored, for repairing the pier when the waves broke it. Don went straight into a dark gap between the blocks, and dragged Harry after him. And then Don stopped, and Harry realised he was in the best air-raid shelter in Tynemouth. Six feet of granite over his head, and solid granite on three sides, and on the fourth a parapet of huge blocks, just low enough to peer over.

"Good dog," he whispered. "Good dog," and fondled the dog's ears. Don was shaking so hard he made Harry shake in sympathy. Harry remembered something his dad had said about dogs in air raids. They suffered terribly with their ears, because they could hear ten times better than people. The sounds were ten times as loud to them. He pulled off one of his jumpers, folded down the dog's ears, and wrapped the jumper round them hard. The dog seemed to like it; it snuggled in.

And then the Castle guns fired, and it was like the end

of the world. The world cracked apart four times; Harry's head seemed to crack apart four times. His ears hurt, physically *hurt*. Like earache.

He remembered the government issuing ear-plugs. Everyone had laughed at the idea of the little rubber ear-plugs, on their bit of string, that you carried in your gas-mask case, if you still carried your gas-mask case, which hardly anyone ever did these days, only kids with soppy mams.

He wished he had them now. But... something... hold the dog with one hand, scrabble in his pockets with the other. Bit of paper; bus ticket. He shoved it into his mouth and chewed it frantically. When it was soggy enough, he worked it into two lumps, and pushed one piece into each of his ears.

The Castle guns fired again. But it was much better now; only half as bad. Didn't *hurt*. He shoved the bits of bus ticket even further in. Then peered with interest over his high bulwark. He'd never been out in an air raid before; he'd always been cowering down in the shelter, like a rat in a hole. Mam hadn't even let him look out of the shelter door, unless it had been quiet for ages.

He thought it was the grandest firework display he'd ever seen. High above, great chains of blue lights hung, lighting the whole sky. They swung; they drifted across each other like swathes of stars. These must be the "chandeliers" Dad had talked about; dropped by the bombers to light their target.

The ack–ack men at South Shields must be trying to shoot them out. Long streams of tracer shells, yellow and red, climbed slowly into the sky from behind South Shields pier. They made the blue lights rock and swing harder, but they didn't put them out. Then the Castle guns fired again, making Don flinch; making a pattern of four bright stars in the sky that burnt holes in your eyes, so that wherever you looked afterwards, there were four black holes in what you looked at. And it all smelt like Guy Fawkes night.

It was… grand. Grand like a thunderstorm, if you were out in it, and not afraid of being hit by lightning. It made Harry feel huge, as huge as the sky.

And then he saw the German bomber, clear and sharp as a minnow in a pond, caught in a cone of no less than five searchlights. It wriggled, glistened like a minnow, a minnow with a shiny nose and tiny crosses on its wings, a minnow trying to escape out of a giant hand. But the giant hand of light held it, twist and turn though it might. Then every gun on Tyneside seemed to be firing at it. Again and again, it vanished in the scatters of blinding flashes. Harry's eyes seemed as full of black holes as Mam's collander. But when the flashes had gone, the tiny plane was still there, twisting and turning and getting bigger. It didn't seem to be going anywhere any more, just wriggling, trying to escape.

And then there was a streak of fire. Then a comet, a shooting star of brilliant yellow, heading out to sea, down to the sea. Down and down and down, brighter and brighter and brighter, better than a two-shilling rocket. And then it burst into a brilliant shower of blue lights, that were caught by the wind and drifted and went out, all but one that glowed all the way down to the dark water.

The guns were silent, so you heard the hiss it made as it hit the sea; heard the people cheering, all the way over the dark water, in South Shields.

He hugged the dog. "We got one, boy, we got one." It was better than North Shields football team scoring a goal. In the silence, the dog thumped its tail against his leg, and licked his hand.

And then the next wave of Jerries came *vroomahing* in.

It was dawn before the Jerries stopped coming, and the all-clear went. He and the dog came out of their deep, deep shelter. The dog stretched, fore and aft, sniffed an upturned boat and peed against it. Harry, walking on what felt like two wooden legs, watched it with great fondness. Don was wonderful. He'd heard the bombers coming, long before the siren went; he'd found the best shelter. Above all, he'd been close to the dog, to its furry warm bulk. The dog had been closer to him than Mam had been, let alone Dad.

He thought he and the dog made a pretty good team. He sat on his upturned boat, and watched the dog sniffing around the beach. Nice to sit in peace and quiet, listening to the little waves plopping on the sand, after the great storm of the night.

But today, Sunday, they had to move on. Before someone noticed him on the beach on Monday morning, and caught him as a truant from school. Before the food ran out. Before the dog went through again what he had gone through last night.

Away. Up the coast. To where there were no people to bother them. To where there was plenty of food.

He knew he wasn't thinking very straight. He needed more sleep. He called to the dog, lured it to him with its share of cold sausage and chips. Then got it through the hole, under the boat, and in a little while they were both sound asleep.

Chapter Five

He started awake, and pushed back the blankets. He was very hot, and there was a small of melting tar, and, worst of all, voices all around him. And the dog was gone.

He must have slept too long. It was Sunday afternoon. On Sunday morning, the beach was empty, except for a few men walking their dogs. But on Sunday afternoons in summer, even in wartime, it filled up with families out for the day. People were sitting with their backs against his boat, blocking out the strip of sunshine. Until they went home, he was trapped. And they usually didn't go home till about six o'clock.

And where was the dog? He could see the place where it had scrabbled out. How long had it been gone? Where had it gone? Had it gone for good? There was nothing he could do. He couldn't scramble out after it, in full view of everybody. It wasn't that he was *afraid* of the people sitting round; it was more a terrible embarrassment at making a fool of himself, of being stared at when he was all dirty and sweaty and peculiar-looking. And his Cousin Elsie, or somebody else he knew might be sitting there.

All he could do was push back the blankets and lie there, and munch another soggy mass of cold chips, and worry about the dog. It was more horrible than being in the shelter during an air raid.

It was the voices that soothed him in the end. The family sitting against the boat, at least, were strangers. A mum and dad, three kids and a granny. They had rough accents; they must come from further up the river. Somewhere like Byker. When the granny said, "I've lived in Byker all me life, and I've never seen anything like *that* in all my born days," it cheered him slightly that he had guessed right.

He sort of lost himself in the life of the family. Bossy mum, idle dad.

"Why don't you play cricket with the bairns, George? They're bored stiff!"

"Why, there's no room to play cricket, hinny. There's not room to swing a cat. Don Bradman hisself couldn't play cricket here."

"Well, do *something* with them!"

"Woman, Aah slave six days a week at the North Eastern Marine, an' even God rested on the seventh day."

"There's our Edith throwing sand in Sammy's eyes again. Stop it, our Edith, or you'll feel the back o' my hand. Cannit ye get them an ice-cream, George? Aah could do wi' one meself."

"Ice-cream? Hinny, there's a war on."

"There's a feller at the top o' the bank…"

"Bloody Italian black marketeer… you don't know what they put in them things. Vaseline an' hair-cream an' anything else they can lay their hands on… would poison a dog."

"Mam, tell our Edith to stop it."

"Our Edith…!"

It was like going back into another life.

And soon there was some good news.

"Mam, this dog's lost. It's starving. Look, it's putting its paw up, asking. It's begging."

"Gerraway, Alsatians can't beg. They're too big."

"It's hungry. Give it that piece of pie Gran dropped in the sand."

"Oh, here y'are then. Anything for peace. D'you think that dog is lost, George?"

Harry tensed up with terror.

"No, it's not lost, hinny. It's gorra collar. It's just on the cadge. I've watched it cadging off people for the last hour. It's doin' all right. Whoever starves, it won't be that dog. C'mere, boy. Have a sandwich. Best spam."

"Get it away. I don't like Alsatians, they're savage."

"'Bout as savage as a new-born lamb. Look, he's rolling over to have his tummy tickled."

Harry listened for a little while longer to the dog cadging food round the beach. It struck him that Don had more talents than he'd imagined. Don was indeed doing all right.

Then he dozed off again. He could just sleep and sleep these days. Must be the heat.

He was wakened by the dog's wet nose, nudging him forcefully in the neck. He came to with a start, worrying about the people. But there was silence outside. When he peered out, the beach was empty. It was later than he wanted it to be. The sun was already dropping towards the cliff top. Night was coming, and with the night, the bombers.

He packed up quickly, shaking the sand out of the blankets. But he took time to wash his face and hands with the anti-flea soap. You had to have a clean face. The water freshened him up. He was busting to go to the toilet, but he held out till he got to the toilet by the bus station.

There was a bus in, going up the coast to Blyth. And he found he had plenty of loose change in his pocket. The driver and conductor had got out, to have a smoke under the clock-tower so he had time to get Don nicely settled, on a tight lead before the conductor dimped his fag and came aboard.

"Where to, young feller-me-lad?"

"Single. All the way," Harry said vaguely.

"Fourpence." The man handed him his ticket, and eyed his luggage. "Been out for the day?"

"On the beach. Camping."

"By God, it's grand to be young." The man left him and went to tend the passengers upstairs.

The bus started, and swung out round the clock-tower. Harry's heart gave a sudden lurch. He was glad to get away from the bombers, and from anybody who might recognise him. But this was home, for the last time. There was Bertorelli's, where they'd come down on a Saturday night for an ice-cream, even in the depths of winter, and then back home by bus, to hear "Inspector Hornleigh Investigates" on the radio.

He was off for pastures new. He swallowed several times, and took a firm grip on Don's collar.

Chapter Six

"This is as far as we go, sonny Jim," said the conductor. "Unless you want to go back to Tynemouth. Where d'you live?"

God, adults got suspicious so quickly. Harry had been dozing, but he had the sense to say, "Across the river." That was all he knew about Blyth; that it had a river. It was ten miles from home, and he'd never been there in his life.

"You'll just catch the last ferry," said the conductor and nodded his head instinctively in a certain direction. Harry grabbed his stuff, all of a shake, and set off in the direction the man had nodded. As he set off, he heard the conductor say to the driver, "Some folks have no sense, letting their bairns wander round this time of night wi' the air raids and all."

It *was* late. The bus seemed to have taken forever. The sun was gone; it was getting dark. He began to hurry. There was no point spending the night here. Blyth was bombed as often as Tynemouth; there were a lot of gaps in the streets of houses. And his mam said Blyth was full of roughs and drunks. He knew he was heading for the river all right, because of the towering dockside cranes. But the river was the roughest part of any town.

And as he turned down the ferry landing, he met two roughs. Men in dirty caps. He didn't like the way they stopped, and watched him approach. The way they filled the whole footpath, blocking his way.

"By, that's a grand dog ye've got there. A grand expensive dog."

"Worth a pretty penny, that dog. Where did ye find him? Is he lost?"

"What ye got in the case, laddy? Show us what you got in the case! We're policemen."

"You're not policemen," said Harry, with a desperate defiance. "You've got no uniforms."

"Special constables, we are!"

"Aye. *Very* special."

They laughed together in a nasty way.

"Plain-clothes men."

"Aye, *very* plain-clothes men. Give us that attaché case,

son. I reckon you've got something *stolen* concealed in there."

"If it's not stolen now, it soon will be." They laughed again, and one man reached for the case, as Harry backed away against the wall.

The next second, Don's leash ripped out of Harry's hand, so hard he felt his palm had been burnt.

Don's black muzzle and huge teeth closed round the reaching hand.

The man fell down, screaming in pain. "Joe, help me, help me, for Christ's sake help me."

Joe kicked at the dog; kicked it in the hind leg.

Don yelped, let go, and went for the second man's face. The sounds he was making were unbelievable, like a wild beast. Harry couldn't believe it was happening. The second man fell down.

Then the next thing he knew was that the two men were on their feet and running, with Don in hot pursuit, barking like a fiend. He vanished round the corner, then came back after a minute, the same old friendly Don as ever, wagging his tail.

Harry grabbed the trailing leash and ran for the ferry. He never knew how he gabbled out his request for a ticket, to the man in the ticket office.

"Steady on, son," said the man, nodding at the ferry. "They won't go without you."

As the gap of dark water widened, between him and the men, Harry looked down at Don. Harry was shaking and trembling so much himself, he could hardly hold the leash and the attaché case. But Don seemed quite calm, not even panting. As Harry watched, he nosed for a flea on his hairy flank, making a vigorous gnawing sound. It seemed all part of a day's work to him.

The far side of the river was quieter. They were soon out of town and into the countryside, full of hawthorn hedges and rows of electricity pylons. He could hear, in the dark, the sea not far away. The sound of the waves soothed him. It was time to look for shelter for the night. Every time you got out of a mess, there was something else to worry about.

They seemed to walk a long way, with nothing but hedges. There seemed no way down to the sea, no hope of an upturned boat. Then something loomed up, as big as a house, shaped like a house. No lights showing. Harry walked up to it, and felt it in the dark. He felt a tight strand of rope, and a lot of soft hay.

A haystack.

Dad had talked about sleeping in a haystack, when he was a lad.

Why not? There seemed to be a cave where someone had broken into the stack. Lined with soft hay.

It was enough. The stack was even thick enough to stop falling shrapnel.

They sat side by side in the cave, and shared the second-to-last packet of sausage and chips. They should have tasted awful, but neither of them could get enough.

Mam had always said that hunger made the best sauce.

Harry was too tired even to undo the blankets. He just pulled hay over the pair of them. Dad had always said you could sleep as snug as a bug in a rug, in a haystack.

It was warm; only it made your face prickle and your nose tickle. He heaved up the pack of blankets and made a pillow out of it.

They slept.

The dog growled once. Harry had no idea what time it was, but he heard the German bombers, far away, in the direction he had come from. Dreamily he watched flashes that he knew must be bombs and guns over Tynemouth. But all far away. He turned over and slept again.

He wakened, warm as toast. The dog slept on, just whuffled in its dream. Its paws moved softly on the hay, as if it was dreaming it was running. Harry got up quietly, so as not to disturb it, and covered it over with the hay again. Seemed the kind thing to do. Then he walked away from the haystack and looked towards the sea, and yawned and stretched and surveyed the lovely morning. The sky was blue, pale blue, from horizon to horizon again. The sea glittered in millions of points of light, under where the sun was. There were white gulls circling over the beach; their calls came faint to his ears. It felt blissy, like the first morning of holiday on the farm at Gilsland, where they had gone every year, even after the war started. It was still cool, and everything smelt good. He wondered what Mr Gilbey, the farmer at Gilsland, was doing at this moment. Would he have finished milking the cows? Harry always got up early and helped with the cows. The smell of them, all steamy and grassy, the smell of the warm streaming milk, spurting into the shining bucket, the slow swish of tails and sound of munching. And Mr Gilbey, singing strange Methodist hymns slowly as he milked.

"When I... spurt... survey... the wondrous... spurt... Cross."

He liked Mr Gilbey; he liked farmers; he liked helping. So when he heard the distant sound of a tractor on the road, he turned to greet it. You always said good morning to people you met in the country, even when you'd never seen them before; it was not like in town.

The tractor approached, the farmer on it getting slowly bigger. He resolved from a series of coloured blobs, and Harry could see he looked quite like Mr Gilbey, with a long-sleeved collarless shirt, and an open waistcoat over it, and a shapeless bulging cap on his head. Harry waved timidly, because it could almost have been Mr Gilbey (though of course it couldn't be). He smiled as he waved.

The tractor stopped. The farmer got down, leaving the engine running. Stooped to pick up a large pair of old leather gauntlets from where the driving pedals were, and walked up to Harry briskly.

"Morning," said Harry. It was what you said in the country. He wondered what the farmer wanted. He couldn't be lost on his own farm; maybe he wanted some help with the harvest; Mr Gilbey always did. Maybe he would pay, or at least give harvest meals of sweet cold tea and apple pie.

"You little sod," said the farmer. "I'll teach you to mess around in my haystack." He raised the hand with the gauntlets in it, and brought it slashing down on Harry's face.

Harry fell down. He managed to yelp, "Please, mister," and then the farmer hit him with the gauntlets again. He tasted blood in his mouth; he held his arms up to protect his face. He rolled around on the ground, trying to get away from the blows. They went on and on and on, on the back of his head, on his shoulders, in his kidneys as he arched his back. His head spun, he couldn't think any more, he was just pains... he yelled and yelled for mercy.

And then it stopped. And somebody else was yelling. Harry looked around wildly. The farmer was standing, just standing. He had dropped the gauntlets, and was clutching his big hairy bare arm. And there was blood trickling down through his fingers.

And Don was standing between him and Harry, crouching, back hunched, teeth bared in a snarl. Don growled, low and awful.

The farmer looked insane. His small blue eyes were popping; his mouth was wide open, showing gaps in his teeth, and his cheeks were covered with whiskers where he hadn't shaved for a week.

Then he gave a yell of rage. "I'll settle your hash, you murderous bastard," he yelled at Don. He made for the tractor at great speed, and picked something up from where he had picked the gauntlets. Something long and shiny.

A double-barrelled shotgun. Harry knew it was, because Mr Gilbey had carried one on his tractor, at harvest time, for potting the rabbits that came out of the last of the corn. Harry leapt to his feet in terror; the farmer was going to shoot Don. He flung himself at the farmer.

"Please, mister, no, no."

The farmer gave him one push that knocked him flat. As Harry got up, the farmer broke open the gun, and put two fat red shells into it, and turned towards Don.

"Mister," screamed Harry, running at him again, trying to get between the gun and Don.

The farmer roughly pushed him away again, against the tractor seat. Harry put out his hand to save himself, and his hand closed round a long piece of wood, a fence-post or something, that was lying on the floor of the tractor.

Harry saw the farmer raise his gun and point it at Don, who was standing looking totally baffled.

Harry's arms just moved of their own accord. He grabbed the fence-post with both hands, raised it high above his head, and hit the farmer. He meant to hit him on the head, on his bulgy cap; but he missed and hit him in the small of the back.

The farmer gave a terrible yell, and fell down. The gun went off along the ground, raising an enormous cloud of dust and grass, cutting a long swathe through the stubble of the field. But Don was no longer anywhere near. Don was off and running, his ears down.

There was a silence. Then the farmer slowly turned his head.

"Christ, kid... I think you've broken me back." He didn't look insane now; he looked very pale and ill and feeble. The freckles stood out on his nose like spots of blood. He tried to raise himself on his hands, managed about six inches, and fell back. "Kid, help me," he said. He had little sandy eyelashes on thick white eyelids. Harry hated him. He was a disgusting object. He'd tried to kill Don, and now he was pleading like a baby. But he'd try to kill Don again, given half a chance…

"Get lost!" shouted Harry. He turned away and grabbed his blankets and attaché case, and ran off down the road. Don, thinking it was a game, came racing past him.

"Kid," shouted the farmer desperately. "Kid." He shouted many times, but Harry just kept on running.

Quarter of a mile further on, at the bend in the road, he looked back.

The farmer had managed to haul himself to his feet against the tractor, but was just standing there.

At least his back *wasn't* broken.

Harry ran on, reached a crossroad, and took the turning for Newbigin-by-the-Sea. His dad had told him about Newbigin; it was a fishing port. It didn't seem a place that a farmer would go. Soon after he crossed the River Wansbeck, he left the road and headed down to the sea.

He found what he was looking for; an old upturned boat on the beach, bleached grey with age and splitting at the seams. Making sure nobody was watching he got the dog under it, and tied him firmly to a thwart, by his lead. They lay there for the rest of the day, while Harry watched through the cracks for farmers and policemen. There wasn't a sign of either. Only one old man, beachcombing for sea-coal, who went home with a full dripping sack, when the sun had begun to set.

It was the smell of real fish and chips, wafted on the northeast breeze from Newbigin that finally lured Harry out after dark. He left the dog tied up, and followed his nose till he found the chip shop. The shop was nearly empty, and the old lady behind the counter was so busy chatting to her crony that she served him without a glance. He got another bottle of Tizer too.

The fish was smashing; but then Newbigin was a fishing village where the boats still went out every day, for rock salmon and rock turbot. The dog enjoyed his fish as well.

On the edge of sleep, Harry thought how right it felt, to be bedding down under a boat again. With the dog. It felt like the only way he had ever lived now. Other bits of him seemed to have dropped off during the day. He tried to think of Dad and Mam and Dulcie and the old days, but the pictures wouldn't come. But he didn't worry. They were buried somewhere, deep and safe in his mind. He'd be able to think about them again. Some day. For now he had the sound of the sea, and a full belly, and warm blankets. And Don. And for the first time, that was enough.

Chapter Seven

The rain caught them on the move. They were travelling by night now, since the business with the farmer. Harry's fear of farmers and policemen was very great.

The rain didn't catch Harry without warning. There was a warning in the change of sounds, in the silence. Every noise came to him as clear as a bell, as they struggled along the fringe of the beach in the dark. A dog barking; voices in the kitchen of a fisherman's cottage; the very breathing of the sea. And the silences in between were cushioned, velvety.

And then there was a warm damp pressure on his left cheek. He knew that rain was coming. But there was nowhere to run to. No upturned boats, no abandoned sheds, not even a shallow cave in the low cliff. Nothing. He tried to hurry in the dark, but that just meant he tripped up more often.

The stars were wiped out one by one, starting with the ones in the west. When half the stars were gone, the first huge dollop of rain smacked him in the face.

He stood, for a moment, full of rage and despair.

"No," he shouted. "Oh, no." But there was no one to hear, no one to help. All he could do was press on.

The dollops came more often, and then they came in a drumming roar on the sand. It was like having a hose-pipe turned on you. His hair settled in streaks across his eyes, dribbling slightly salty water straight into his mouth. The water began to get inside the collar of his raincoat, then it ran down his back. It broke in through the raincoat at his shoulders, where the strap of the blankets pressed, making his goose-fleshed skin crawl and shudder. Soon it was running down his legs, and sloshing in his shoes, and everything was sodden. There came a time when he gaspingly knew that he couldn't get any wetter. His clothes began to chafe his flesh like wet ropes; the handle of the attaché case grew too slippery to hold, so he kept on dropping it. He knew the blankets must be getting sodden too, for they grew heavier and heavier, and the strap cut more and more.

Don just plodded along beside him, occasionally shaking himself to get the water out of his coat.

Everything was melting away. All his plans, all his hopes, all his sense. Except a stubborn voice that went on telling him to keep going, keep going...

He would have walked straight past the place in his misery; he had given up looking around, the rain beat in his eyes too much. But the dog stopped, and looked left, and sniffed. So Harry looked too.

There was a dip in the low cliff, a sheltered tiny cove with a little leaping stream, and what looked like three or four small abandoned railway carriages, without their wheels, dotted about. There were no lights in them; no smoke coming from their chimneys. The night sky showed through their big windows.

A last savage burst of energy drove him up the bank of the stream, slipping and slithering. His foot went into the stream and didn't feel any wetter, though the mud on the bottom sucked at his shoe treacherously, and he almost lost it. Then he was in the lee of the first carriage; the rain stopped battering in his face, and he came to his senses.

He tried a door on the first carriage, but it was locked. He tried all that carriage's doors; they were all locked. But he could see, through the carriage windows, tantalising objects in the gloom. Beds and heaps of blankets, a cast-iron stove, a box of knives and forks.

He ran across and tried the next carriage. That was locked too. But he saw deckchairs piled, and aluminium pots and pans on a paraffin stove, even a pile of foodtins in an open cupboard. There was shelter in there, and dry blankets and food. So close. Only a sheet of glass away.

He crossed to the third carriage, and the wind and rain hit him with renewed ferocity, so he staggered and fell down. His mind was a roaring turmoil. He would die... the dog would die. They had a right to live... as much right as these people who owned these holiday railway carriages. They had another home somewhere. They weren't out in this storm. He made up his mind he would smash the glass on the last carriage, if it was locked.

The door opened as he turned the handle. He splashed back for his bundles.

"Come on, boy!"

The dog needed no second telling. They were out of the storm with the door shut in a flash. The storm was only screaming round the corners of the carriage, and the rain lashing harmlessly against the great windows, and drumming on the roof. The whole place smelt musty, as if nobody had lived there for a long time.

There was a great brass paraffin lamp, hanging from the ceiling. He knew the sort; his gran had once had one just like it. He swung it; plenty of paraffin glugged inside. He lifted out the glass funnel carefully, because he was shivering all over. Remembered which way to turn the little brass wheels, so the wicks came up, instead of vanishing down inside.

He groped the attaché case open, and felt for the matches he'd had so long ago. They were still dry; it was a good attaché case. But his hands were wet, and that might spoil the matches. He found something in the dark to dry them on; it took a long time to dry them; the rain seemed to have soaked right inside them, as if they were a sodden dishcloth.

A golden light sprang up and lit the carriage. And he immediately panicked about the blackout. But there were thick, thick curtains. He felt their dusty dryness as he drew them. Safe.

It was then he saw the piece of writing, propped up against a flower vase on the little table. It was on a piece of thick white cardboard, probably cut from a shoebox. It said,

> *To the lost traveller.*
>
> *You are welcome here, friend. The door is not locked. Sleep if you wish. Eat what you need. We are glad that, even in wartime, we could leave you something. Go on your way in the morning refreshed.*

Please leave things as you found them for the next person in need. Pay if you can for what you have had, but if you cannot, do not worry. Pray for us, as we will pray for you.

Jack, Harriet, Susan and Shirley.

PS. We hope you will be as happy here as we have always been.

PPS. Spare paraffin in the can outside.

There was a framed photograph by the side of the note, propped up on its little leg at the back. It was of a vicar in his dog-collar and his wife and two little girls. They were all smiling at the camera, in a broad friendly way. They looked nice.

Harry stared around. The carriage was just one big room, except for a plank wall with a door at one end; beyond the door was a little table with an enamel bowl and ewer, and a lot of hooks on the wall. All the railway seats were gone; but there was a wood-stove with paper and sticks and coal, a big table with plates, easy chair and bunk-beds made up with sheets.

It was weird, like Goldilocks in the house of the three bears. He was almost afraid to touch anything, except the family kept smiling at him from the photograph, as if urging him on.

A big shiver warned him to get out of his sopping clothes; besides, they were dripping on the floor, making puddles. He tossed them down in the enamel basin and wrapped himself in a brown blanket. After that, there was the dog to dry, the stove to light, a huge tin of baked beans to open and share. So much to do, and he was so *weary*. But at last he could crawl into a bunk, leaving all his wet things to steam on chairs round the glowing stove. It was on the verge of sleep that he remembered the bargain he had struck.

"Please, God, keep Jack, Harriet, Susan and Shirley safe."

He had a fleeting image of their smiling faces as he lay with his eyes shut.

Then he had an image of his own house bombed flat, smelling of gas and burning with little low blue flames.

God didn't seem to have anything to say in reply.

But then God, in Harry's experience, never had.

He stayed two days; two days of endless rain. He stayed warm and snug. He got everything nice and dry, though his trousers seemed to have shrunk a bit. His old mates would've said they were flying at half-mast.

He ate the food; Spam, corned beef and endless baked beans. Even tinned peaches, which he hated and the dog wouldn't touch. He felt very guilty, every tin he ate, but what could he do? Every tin he opened, he looked at the family for reassurance. They went on smiling at him. He seemed to get to know them very well. He read all the girls' comics. The little one must have read *Puck*. The eldest seemed to like boys' comics, like *Hotspur* and *Adventure*. The mother had read *Woman's Weekly*, but all the vicar had left behind was a big black Bible and a copy of *The Pilgrim's Progress*. By the second afternoon he had read everything else, and was reduced to looking up the dirty bits in the Bible, where so-and-so lay with so-and-so. Then he looked at the ever-smiling family on the table, and felt deeply ashamed.

He found *The Pilgrim's Progress* not much easier. But there was one bit that took his fancy.

"I saw a man clothed with rags… with his face from his own house… and a book in his hand and a great burden on his back. I looked and I saw him open the book and read therein; and as he read, he wept and trembled… and broke out with a lamentable cry saying, 'What shall I do?'"

That was his own state really, wasn't it? It was a slight comfort to realise people had been in this kind of jam before; that there was a name for it.

"I'm a pilgrim," he said out loud, liking the word. "Pilgrim."

★ ★ ★

The third morning dawned bright and clear. He got up the moment he wakened, the moment he realised the rain had stopped. He flung back the curtains, and the old blue sky was back, horizon to horizon. There was a mist out to sea, that meant it was going to be a really hot day. The dog pleaded urgently to go out, relieved itself, then began running madly in circles round the carriages. It was ready for the road, and so was he. But he left with care; piled his bags outside first, then cleaned out the stove, made the bed, swept and dusted. He thought it looked pretty good; just like it had been, when he arrived. He wrote a note saying, "Thank you. A pilgrim." He hovered, undecided whether to leave a ten-shilling note under the photograph, or a pound. In the end he settled for a pound. he had eaten an awful lot, and it was on the ration.

He was just picking up the attaché case, when he saw the old man coming up from the beach. He was not in the least afraid of the old man. He had silver hair, and walked painfully with a stick. A puff of wind would have blown him away. It would be hours before the old man could get to the police…

"Morning," said the old man, coming up to the door. "That's a grand dog you've got." The old man's eyes were very sharp. Took in Harry's face, his clothes, his luggage, and the pound note on the table, all in one glance. "Thanks for leaving the pound note."

"I was here two days an' three nights," said Harry. "We ate an awful lot…"

"That's all right, son. And you left the place nice too. Good lad." There was such… gratitude in the old man's voice that Harry grew bold.

"Is this your railway carriage?"

"No. It was my lad's."

"The vicar? Jack?"

"Aye, Jack. God rest him!"

"Is… is he *dead*?" Harry's voice rose to a squeak he couldn't control.

"Aye. And his missus. And the bairns. In the bombing at Newcastle. A year gone. They all went together. One little bomb on the vicarage. The houses each side were scarce touched."

"But… but…" Harry stared round the carriage. "They seemed so…" He couldn't get it out.

"Alive? Aye, they're here. If they're anywhere. That's why I keep the place on. They bought it to come and be near me, on their holidays. They were that happy here. Always laughing."

"I'm sorry," said Harry.

The old man put his hand on Harry's arm. "Don't be sorry, son. Ye're the first customer we've had. Aah used to reckon they were mad, leaving the door unlocked when they weren't here, an' that notice on the table. But Jack always said that anyone of ill-will could soon smash a door or a window open, and he'd be in a rage by the time he'd got inside. Whereas if he was welcomed, he'd respect the place... ye've proved my Jack was right after all, son. Thank you. It gives me the strength to go on wi' things, here. God bless you, whoever you are." Tears stood out in his old eyes. "What's your name, son? I'm going to write it in the book – the first name."

"Harry Baguely."

"And might I ask where you're headed?" asked the old man, very gently.

"Just... up the coast," said Harry. "I'm a pilgrim."

"Oh, ye're gannin to Holy Island – Lindisfarne?"

"Yes," said Harry. Though he hadn't decided till that very moment. Now, somehow, he *had* to go to Lindisfarne.

"God bless you, Harry Baguley," said the old man. "You and your dog."

Tears grew in Harry's own eyes. He suddenly felt he wanted to tell the old man everything about the bombing. It was like a great weight of water inside him, held back by a thin, thin dam. But the old man had enough troubles of his own. And the old man was happy now, in a way. Harry couldn't bear to spoil his happiness, to let all the misery inside himself loose in the world.

"Tara," he said abruptly, before he broke down. Shouldered his blankets, picked up his case and went.

But he turned and waved, before he was out of sight. The old man was sitting on the step of the carriage, lighting his pipe. He waved back.

Chapter Eight

The light was failing as they came off the rocks and into sight of Druridge Bay.

That was always the worst time, when the light failed. It was all right in the morning, when the sun was shining and the whole day lay ahead. It was nice to doze and watch the dog swimming, in the heat of the noonday sun. But getting dark had always been home-time, draw the curtains and wait for Dad to come from work time. The time Mam began to cook supper.

Druridge Bay was five miles of sand-dunes, low cliffs and empty sand. Not a thing stirred in the whole long curve of it. Five weary miles of nothing. And he had nothing to eat again. He stared around bleakly. Out to sea, some buoys and floats bobbed meaninglessly. Druridge Bay, Dad once said, was a bombing range for the RAF, simply because nobody ever went there. He wondered wearily whether a plane would appear and drop a bomb on him and the dog; it would solve a lot of problems.

But the dog seemed to have found something, under the low, crumbling mud-coloured cliff. The dog was circling and barking. He put on a weary spurt to catch up.

The dog was barking at a very odd building, tucked under the cliff. A long box of a building, like a sagging shed. Fisherman's hut? But surely even the poorest fisherman could do better than this? It was a shed made of patches. Patches of withered plank, of tins hammered flat and nailed on. Patches of corrugated iron, patches of old lino with the pattern still on it. But all painted with black tar, against the wind and rain. And at the far end, a thin stovepipe chimney, from which came smoke and… the smell of cooking fish. It must be the smell of the cooking that was making the dog bark.

He was still about fifty yards away, when a door in the patchwork swung open, and a figure emerged and flung a piece of what looked like wood at the dog. It flew straight and true, and hit the dog on the backside. Don gave a yelp, and fled to a safe distance.

"Hey," shouted Harry. "That's *my* dog."

The figure turned. It was very tall and remarkably thin, with pale bare feet, and trousers that finished raggedly halfway up its legs. All in black it was, with a long thin neck and long thin face, and hair that glinted silver in the last of the light. It looked eerie, like a ghost or a scarecrow. But it said, in a pettish voice, "You should keep your dog under better control then!"

"It's cos he's hungry."

"You shouldn't keep a dog if you can't afford to feed it."

It was a voice like a scolding old granny's, when she comes to her front door to tell you not to make so much noise playing. But it looked like a man. His hair was cut all ragged behind, and his face was so old, even the wrinkles had wrinkles. But he moved as quick as a kid, a nervous kid.

"What's yer name?"

"Harry Baguley." There was no harm in telling this oddball. Nobody would ever believe what *he* said.

"And what you doin' round here at this time o' night, Harry Baguley? If your parents had any sense you'd be in bed, or doin' your homework."

"They're dead," said Harry. "Killed in the bombing." This bloke was so weird, you really could tell him anything.

"So you're an orphan?" said the figure. "So am I. I suppose you'd better come in then."

Harry hesitated; remembered Dad's warning about

going with strangers. But this bloke sounded reluctant, as if he didn't want to ask Harry in really. As if he didn't want to be bothered, but he felt it was his duty.

"Can I bring the dog in?"

"If it shuts up, and minds its manners."

It was dark inside the strange hut. There was only the light of the burning stove, which appeared to be cut out of a big thick oil drum, and a couple of lighted wicks which floated in a yellow liquid, in rusty tin cans. The smell of burning rotten fish was overpowering. Harry felt a bit sick.

"Sit down." The man pointed to an unpainted keg, stamped "Danish butter". Harry sat, and stared round. The walls were hung with all kinds of things. Three ship's lifebelts, a huge unlit ship's lantern, the broken rudder of a fishing boat, rusty saws and hammers. The man followed Harry's eyes.

"All from the sea," he said, with a strange pride. "All from the sea. I am an orphan, but the sea is my father and my mother."

Don began nosing around.

"Keep that dog still, or you'll have to go," shouted the man suddenly and shrilly. Harry, hearing a sudden patter of rain on the roof, grabbed Don's collar, and said carefully, "What's *your* name?"

"Joseph Kielty. Everybody knows me round here, for

miles around. I used to be a clerk at Smith's Dock, afore my mother died, God rest her. Then I came here. Do you want some fish stew?"

"Yes, please," said Harry. He didn't know which was worse, feeling ravenous, or feeling sick from the smell of burning fish. But when the fish stew was ladled out of a pot on the stove, and given to him with an incredibly battered spoon, it tasted marvellous. Don sniffed at the bowl hungrily, hopefully.

"Have you got something for my dog?" asked Harry cautiously.

"Does he eat raw fish?"

"He'll eat anything."

The man produced a large whole fish from somewhere, and lured the dog outside with it, and slammed the door. "I'm not having him making a mess in here."

They both listened in silence to the sounds of chewing outside the door. Then Harry said, "How long you lived here?"

"Since afore the last war. The last war was none of my business. Neither is this one. I thought the Germans might be going to land here a couple o' years ago, but they seem to have changed their minds now. Want to listen to the news?"

Without waiting for Harry to say yes, he swung round

and turned on a large old-fashioned radio, with a proud flourish. "That radio's the one thing the sea didn't give me. I bought it second-hand at Hardy's in Amble. I bought it with the money I got for the fish. It runs on batteries. I buy them with money from the fish too."

They listened in silence to Bruce Belfrage reading the news. The news wasn't very good, as usual. The Eighth Army were retreating in the Western Desert. The Russians were retreating round Smolensk. The RAF had sustained "comparatively light" losses, bombing Germany. The man switched off. "Must save the batteries. How you goin' to manage, now you're an orphan?"

"Dunno," said Harry warily.

"You can always manage, by the sea," said the man. "I've learnt that the hard way, over thirty years. I'll show you how, if you like. Then you'll have to go away and find your own beach. There's not room for two here on this one. Is that a bargain?"

"That's nice of you," said Harry, and found he meant it.

"Just doin' me bit for the War Effort," said the man. "You'll have to sleep outside though. Wi' the dog. In the shed." And he immediately led Harry to the door, taking the empty bowl off him as he went.

The "shed" was simply one end of the long building, with a wall missing. It was full of propped-up, saltstained planks of wood, old fish boxes and lumps of cork. Don followed, the well-chewed remains of the fish still in his mouth. The wind, getting up, howled round the open shed, blowing in both spots of rain and rifts of hissing dry sand.

"You'll make yourself snug enough here," said the man. "Well, goodnight to you." And he went in and slammed the door hard.

Harry managed to build some kind of shelter for himself and Don, behind the propped-up wood.

A hand shook his shoulder. "Time to get up. Tide's on the turn. Time's a-wasting. Drink this." The man thrust a very chipped enamel mug into Harry's hand. Harry sipped it. He thought it was tea without milk or sugar; it was as bitter as gall, but after he'd drunk it, he felt better. He peered out of his shelter. Dawn was just breaking, a steely slit between grey sky and darker sea. There was a brisk breeze, with rain in it.

Then the man was back, and handing him three straw fish baskets, with handles.

"*That* one's for sea-coal, an' that one's for slank, and that one's for anything interesting you find."

"Like what?"

"You'll see," said the man, striding off, with what seemed to be four straw baskets in each hand.

After two hours, Harry's back was breaking; he was soaked and his knees were caked with sand, and he'd lost all feeling in his hands from cold and wet; they were red and swollen. And yet he was still fascinated. The man stalked the tide-line, bent double all the time, looking as natural as a heron on the hunt for its breakfast. He stalked with a heron-stride; he dipped with his hand like a heron striking. His feet even looked like heron's feet, bony and splayed and grey. And he must have eyes like gimlets. He didn't just find sea-coal (which Harry soon learnt to recognise), and slank (which was a particular kind of seaweed, which the man said was better for you than green vegetables). He found a penny, with the King's head almost worn away by the sea and sand. He found a round rusty tin, still half-full of sweet-smelling tobacco. He found a sodden navy-blue jumper, with one elbow worn out, but it would darn. A baby's dummy, nearly new, a deflated rubber bathing-ring that could be repaired. Two crabs stranded by the tide, a dead flatfish that was sniffed and pronounced still fresh, and a crippled sea-bird that he despatched with one blow of a charred plank, saying it would make supper. But he was most jubilant about some orangey stones, that he said were amber.

"These started," he said, "as lumps o' resin oozing out of a fir tree in Denmark, hundreds and hundreds o' years ago. I gotta piece once wi' a fly caught inside it. All those hundreds of years ago. The feller who comes from Newcastle gave me five bob for that one. They usually make women's beads out of them. But that one wi' the fly was special. It was sent to a museum in America." Then he said, "Not much of a morning. They've not been bombing these last few days. No fish. Come on and I'll give you some breakfast."

They staggered up the beach, carrying loads of charred wood, as well as full bags of sea-coal and slank.

He learnt to live with Joseph; learnt when to stand up for himself, and when to bend.

Joseph had moods. In the morning, he was as cruel and savage as a gull. If the dog got in his way, he would kick it, with those grey iron-hard bare feet. If Harry got in the way, he would kick him too. There was no arguing with Joseph in the mornings; he would get hysterical, screaming at you, so that his spit landed on your face. He would tell you to pack your bags and go.

In the afternoons, especially if it was sunny, he would sing to himself, the old songs of a whole war ago.

"Keep the home fires burning…"

If he found something good in the afternoons, he would caper around like a boy. The afternoon they found the whole keg of butter, three-quarters buried in the sand, he grabbed Harry and waltzed with him half down the beach, working out how many radio batteries the money from the keg would buy.

At the end of the working day, after a mug of the vile tea, he would get dressed up in an old shiny black suit, and even boots, and cycle on his old butcher-boy's bike up to the town of Amble, with his carrier laden with loot for the grocer's and the second-hand shop. It was the only time he ever wore anything on his feet; and a collar and tie as well. He looked almost normal. When he came back, he would get the supper, and tell Harry word for word what he had said to the grocer, and how he'd put one over the second-hand dealer. That was the time to ask him favours. He would even give you things, without being asked. Sometimes the things were useful, like a clasp-knife with blades honed down till they were like sickles. Sometimes they were useless, like a photograph of a little girl in a Victorian sailor-suit.

Later in the evening, he would drink from black bottles, and put his arm around you, and tell you the story of his life, or philosophise.

"Everything's good for something, Harry, everything's good for something. A dead fish has no use for its body, but the seagull that finds it has. A wrecked ship's no good to a sailor, but it's good for firewood. This war's bad for sailors, but it's good for me. I find dead 'uns, you know. Drag 'em above high water, and go for the coastguard. They pay me a pound for every dead 'un. An' when I die, I hope I go on the beach. Good for the fish, good for the gulls. I don't want to lie in no dark hole when I'm dead.

When he started to talk about being dead, it was time to retire to the shed for the night. Lie cuddled up with Don, and listen to Joseph shouting at himself, and at his dead mother, and at God.

And then it was morning again.

You never asked what you were eating with Joseph cooking. But the funny thing was, it always tasted good. And you never got ill. And you learnt so much; it was like being back at school again.

Until the day the bombers came. The British bombers.

They hadn't been on the beach more than two hours, when the first bomber came. Hard up the coast, at zero height, skirting Beacon Point and the Scars: a mutter, a roar, a scream of engines. Tiny bombs dropping from its yellow belly, at the yellow markers floating so peacefully in Druridge Bay. It was a strange bomber to Harry; not one out of the war magazines or aircraft-recognition booklets his dad had had. It had a little solid pointed nose, and two pointed engines, and an oval tailfin. Must be a new sort.

The tiny bombs exploded, sending up plumes of white

foam, and banging Harry's ears painfully. But Joseph was dancing again, waving wildly as the second bomber started its run.

"Tide's coming in. Fresh fish for tea tonight. Run and get boxes, lad. All the boxes you can find."

Harry fetched all the boxes they had. Joseph had obviously given up beachcombing for the day; he just stood and watched and waved as ten bombers came, one after the other.

Then the bay was quiet again. Where were all these marvellous fish?

And then suddenly a wave broke on the shore that was silver. A solid wave of fish, tiny and large and enormous. And all dead. Fish to pick up in handfuls. Fish to fill boxes till they could hold no more. And still the fish came. And still Joseph capered, drunk with joy.

When the fish stopped coming, he put on his suit, and went to Amble to telephone, leaving Harry on guard.

Soon after he returned, a green van came, with three men to load the fish. They stared curiously at Harry, before they paid Joseph, and drove away.

Joseph turned to Harry and said, "Those men asked your name. I think they've gone for the poliss. They don't like you being with me. They think I'm potty." He tapped his head. "They think I'll do bad things to you, because I'm potty." He tapped his head again. "Better go now, Harry. Go and find your own beach. I taught you all I know. The sea will be your mother and father now. Goodbye."

Then he turned and walked away, not up to the shed, but towards his bike and Amble. As he mounted, he shouted, "I didn't see which way you went."

And then he was gone.

And Harry was on the run again.

Chapter Nine

Harry only went about two miles up the beach, and then found a cranny in the crumbling cliffs. He wasn't sure if a policeman would come, or if it was just Joseph's way of finally getting rid of him. But best not to take chances. A policeman was much too big a thing to take risks about. Policemen were final; you couldn't fight policemen.

But he reckoned the police were much too busy to come searching the cliffs. Or plod along the beach without their bikes. They would watch the roads; ask people at their cottage doors whether they'd seen a boy and a dog go by. The best thing was to lie low, till everyone had forgotten about him.

He lay low on a ragged patch of cliff top where the fields

didn't quite come to the cliff edge. He didn't want any bother with farmers either. There was a slightly worn path along the edge of the cliff; but he hid himself from the path in a patch of gorse. Don seemed quite content to lie with him. The sun shone in fits and starts, but it would have been very dull, if it hadn't been for the beach and the sea. Tide was going out, leaving strands of sparkling black sea-coal, and half a ship's lifebelt, and a couple of empty bottles. Higher up, above the high-tide mark, there was plenty of dry seaweed that would make a soft bed for the night, if you shook the sandfleas out of it… he would never be bored beside a beach again, thanks to Joseph.

He let dusk descend before he went on along the cliff path. He didn't wait till total dark, because, although these cliffs weren't very high, he didn't want to fall down them. He was hungry, but he was used to being hungry by this time. He could wait till morning, if he had to.

It was not quite dark when he saw the cottage, right on the edge of the cliff. There was no smoke coming out of the single chimney. And it was a funny place for a cottage to be, somehow. The land seemed to be crumbling under its edge, and it was tilting ever so slightly seawards, as if it might fall down the cliff at any moment. But it wasn't falling apart; it was tilting all together, like a tin toy cottage. It had no garden, and no sign of life.

He crept closer. The windows looked funny, not right somehow. There were slates off the roof, and dusk showed through the rafters. Not much shelter from the rain there. But worth a look. He tiptoed up to it, silently as he could.

He touched the wall. It wasn't brick, he realised with a shock. It was concrete, with bricks just crudely painted on it, and the paint was flaking off, like the old stage scenery at school. The walls were cold smooth concrete, and very thick. And the windows were just painted on as well, and the little blue curtains. In the middle of each painted window was a machine-gun slit.

It was a pillbox, just got up to look like a cottage. Even the pointed roof was a flimsy fake; with a flat concrete roof underneath. That was why it was starting to slide down to the sea all in one piece, without falling apart. A pillbox from 1940, a pillbox for the Home Guard.

The steel door was half-open, and part-buried and jammed in the sand, so it wouldn't close. It had door-panels painted on it, and a number thirteen – somebody's old joke.

He sniffed inside. Just the smell of the sea, covering a faint, dirty dried-out smell, which he knew very well. Somebody, a long time ago, had used the pillbox as a lavatory. That meant that nobody official ever came here any more. This was 1942, and the Home Guard was a joke, because everybody knew that Hitler wasn't coming now.

He went inside, and lit one of the stumps of candle he'd nicked off Joseph. (Well, he was owed something, for loading all that fish.) The floor was thick with sand – two or three inches, blown in by the wind. And there were things left lying, besides the mummified brown curls that were making the faint dirty smell. There was a browned *Daily Mirror* from two months ago – that would come in useful for the loo. And there were bottles, beer bottles, that could be used to store water. And a box that could be broken up for firewood.

But there were other things that baffled him. A pair of sandy snake-like objects, that turned out to be a pair of woman's stockings. And a little gold thing that glinted fat yellow in the candlelight – a cheap earring. What the hell were dressed-up women doing, in a dump like this?

But the great thing he found was a real fireplace, with real ashes in it. Pillboxes weren't supposed to have fireplaces… but he supposed since the fake cottage had to have a chimney, the Home Guard had made the most of it.

It occurred to him that he could make this place very snug. Somebody had already blocked up the machine-gun slits with a mixture of sacking and half-bricks, for some reason…

He suddenly missed the dog. He went to the cliff edge and saw it moving, a dim shape, down on the beach, running between the bands of seaweed, nosing here and there. Don was looking for his supper. Lucky Don.

He didn't do much that night. Just picked up the mummified filth from the sandy floor with paper, and threw it over the cliff. Then he spread his blankets, and lay down listening to the sound of the sea.

Don soon came back, carrying something slimy in his mouth that smelt strongly of fish. To the sound of Don gnawing with gusto, he fell asleep.

The next day was the most exasperating so far. It started all right. He was wakened in the dawn, by the sound of the tide turning; he had all Joseph's habits by this time. He was on the beach straightaway, looking for what the tide had left.

There was plenty of good big sea-coal; but he had no straw baskets to carry it in. He had to leave it in a row of little heaps, till he found a fish box. The fish box was big, and he filled it too full of coal, and it was heavy to carry. By the time he'd carried three boxfuls up the cliff, he was weak and weary.

He tried to dig free the iron door from the sand, so he could close it and keep his things safe. But when he had dug enough sand away, he found the hinges were rusted solid and wouldn't budge. So, by the time the sun was well up, and people might come, he had to bundle up his things and find a hiding place for them in the false roof over the pillbox. Slates kept falling off, revealing his hiding places.

The real trouble was, he didn't know if this was a safe place or not. He didn't know if people still walked here, along the cliff path. Couples with dogs; nosy kids, because it was Saturday morning again.

And even worse, he had nothing to eat. He'd found two dead fish, that smelt all right. He'd topped and tailed and gutted them, as Joseph had taught him. But he didn't dare light a fire to try to cook them until nightfall. Smoke from the chimney in broad daylight would be a dead giveaway. He tried to eat the fish raw, but the feel of it in his mouth made him throw up, bitter strings of gall falling from his mouth on to the sand. He chewed a bit of his pocketful of slank, but it felt like chewing string.

He would have to walk to Amble, and try to get something at a fish and chip shop, before he died of hunger. And he might meet Joseph in Amble, and then there'd be a right row.

He walked along the cliff path, miserable as sin. Don ran before him, obviously well-fed, plume of tail waving, full of the joys of spring. He wished bitterly that he was a dog as well.

It was a mile on that he saw the Bofors anti-aircraft guns,

sticking their long thin muzzles into the sky, out of their circular walls of sandbags. Motionless. All except one, that was going round and round in the most peculiar way. A bit further on, there was a low brick building with sandbags piled up in front of the windows, and a green army truck. But there was no sign of life, except that the one gun kept going round and round. It was too intriguing; he couldn't resist it. He walked up to it, stepping over a very discouraged barbed-wire fence.

The gun stopped circling one way, and began going round the other. In his hungry state, it made him feel quite dizzy.

There was a single soldier, sitting on the seat attached to the gun, whirling his arms so fast on some handle sticking out of the gun that his arms were a blur. He wasn't a very smart-looking soldier; he had his forage-cap shoved under the epaulette on his shoulder, and his overalls were filthy with grease.

As he circled past, he saw Harry standing there, and stopped.

"Hi, son!" He had a friendly lopsided grin, because he had a fag-end, unlit, stuck in one corner of his mouth. "You look like you've lost a shilling and found sixpence. All the cares of the world on your shoulders, on a lovely morning like this?"

"I'm starving," said Harry. What had he got to lose? And the man did have a very friendly grin.

"Doesn't your mam feed you?"

"Bread an' scrape this morning. She's gone to Amble for the week's rations." Even Harry marvelled at what a liar he had become.

"Hard for growing boys," said the man, lighting his fag. "Try our dustbins." He nodded towards the brick building. "Go on, don't look at me like that. It's wicked what they throw away, after a quiet night. When you get a Jerry raid coming over, they get as hungry as hunters, and scoff the lot. But on a quiet night, they sleep right through, and it's all wasted."

"Won't they stop me, over there?"

"All gone down to the airfield for a shower. That's a soldier's dream, that is – a shave, a shower and a shit." He went back to whirling round and round on his gun.

Harry walked across, and opened the dustbin lid, and saw a mountain of white sandwiches, cut thick as doorsteps, but full of corned beef. There was a bit of dirt on the top ones, from the dustbin lid, and somebody had emptied tea-slops on to the ones on the right, but by careful picking, he got a dozen good as new, just a little dry and curling at the edges. He stuffed most of them into his pocket, and bit into the best one.

"There's a better lad," said the soldier kindly, stopping his whirling again. From the faded stripes, almost invisible on his oily sleeve, Harry saw he was a corporal. "Tell you what, son, if you're ever pushed for grub, this is the place to come. They get so many bloody sandwiches here they even look like sandwiches. You get sandwich fights in the barrack room some nights, after they've been boozing in the NAAFI."

"Aren't they scared the Germans might come?"

"Jerry doesn't show his face by daylight any more up here. He knows what's good for him. You know what they've got at Acklington airfield – *Spitfires*. Jerry wouldn't get half-way across the North Sea before the RDF picked him up."

"What's RDF?"

"None of your business – I never said a word." He looked down on the ground. "Hand me up that five-eight spanner, son, will you?"

"What you doing?"

"Easing the tracking-gears. I told the bloody armourer they were stiff, and he had a go at them, but he's bloody useless. You can't hit Jerry if the tracking-gears' stiff as glue. So I'm having a go meself. I used to be a fitter in civvy street. This is my gun. Like to have a try on her?"

"How?" Harry's mouth fell open in amazement and wonder.

"Hop on the seat the other side of her. That's right. Now, you see the handles in front of you? You turn them, the barrel goes up and down. I make the gun go round and round, and you make it go up and down. So we can aim at things. Let's try and get that flock of geese that's flying over." He pointed, and the gun barrel began to turn towards them. But it was too high. Harry twiddled his own pair of handles, and the barrel sadly went even higher.

"Other way, son. You'll soon get the hang of it. Aim through the gun-sight in front of you."

Harry peered through the ring-sight with its crossed wires. Twiddled the handles first one way, then the other, and finally got the rapidly vanishing geese right in the sight.

"Well done," said the corporal. "Only you got to aim well in front of them, to allow the shells you fire time to get to where they are. And you'd have to be a bit sharper than that – the Jerries can fly a bit faster than Canada Geese, and they don't hang about waiting for you."

"Where's the trigger?" asked Harry.

"There, son. But don't touch it, or it might go off. And then the army would dock five quid out of my pay, for wasting a shell."

Harry stared; at the gun's long, long barrel, with its widening tip; at the gleaming racks of brass shells. He had never seen anything so thrillingly evil in his life. He squirmed on the hard metal seat with sheer glee.

"Has it – got a name?"

"I call her Biffie – Biffie the Bofors. She's a good lass; she's knocked bits off a couple of Jerries that won't come back in a hurry." He lit another fag, squinting as the smoke hit his eyes. "I've got a lad just about your age, at home. Twelve are you?"

"Thirteen next birthday."

"Never get to see my lad – he's evacuated to Cornwall. Takes me all me time to get a forty-eight to see me missus. My lad's growing up, an' I never see him. I was teaching him cricket – used to take him to the Oval, to see Wally Hammond play. He'll be a grown man, by the time I get out of this lot. Still, at least I know he's safe. Not like 1940 – he nearly got killed when the Germans burnt the London Docks. In hospital for a month, poor little bleeder."

The corporal suddenly looked quite desperate. So Harry held out his hand and said, "My name's Harry – Harry Baguley. I live down the coast a bit. We got bombed out too."

"Put it here, pard!" The grin came back on the corporal's face. "My name's Arthur Blenkinsop – but you can call me Uncle Artie. All the young un's in the battery do. Here's another flock of geese – d'you fancy another go?"

They whirled round and twiddled the handles and laughed. Harry suddenly felt at home, and terribly happy.

Then Artie got down stiffly, putting his hands to his back and saying, "I'm not as young as I was. I like your dog. What's his name?"

"Don." Artie and Don made friends. Artie seemed to know the right place to tickle a dog, behind the ears.

"Had a dog before the Blitz – ran away an' never came back."

"You can borrow Don, any time you like. He likes the beach an' swimming for sticks." It seemed a ridiculous thing to say, and dangerous. But he liked Artie so *much*.

Artie suddenly patted his pockets, and said, "You wouldn't do me a favour, Harry, would you? I'm clean out of fags, and I've got a lot to do here yet. You wouldn't like to run down to the NAAFI for me – at the airfield? You can borrow my bike, and I'll give you a chit for the NAAFI-wallah."

"With the greatest of pleasure," said Harry, and then blushed because he sounded so pompous.

"Right. I'll lower the saddle for you."

Five minutes later, he was cycling down the road, with Don in joyous pursuit.

He came back even fuller of wonder. The NAAFI was outside the airfield barbed wire, but only just. He'd seen the windsock blowing yellow in the breeze, and the control tower in the distance, and the shapes of sharklike Spitfires in their sandbagged dispersals, with men crawling all over them, and starting up their engines. And there'd been no trouble at the NAAFI, though people had stared as he went in. But the man behind the counter knew Artie. When he read the chitty, he just said, "Bloody Artie. The war would stop if he didn't get his fags."

But when Harry got back to the guns, there was no sign of Artie; and what was much worse, the long brick barrack was full of men. He could see them leaning out of the windows, smoking, and behind, others hitting each other with towels.

He nearly turned and ran on the spot.

But Artie was his friend, and he needed his fags.

It took him all his courage to walk through the door. When he got inside, the noise was deafening. One man was dancing on the end of his bed in only a shirt, and that was waving up round his neck. Harry flicked his eyes away, and was knocked flat by two men having a wrestling-match, swearing at each other with such a flood of language as he'd never heard before. Don leapt to the rescue, barking.

Somebody yelled, "Mind the kid, ye daft buggers."

And then there was a great silence in the hut, and everyone was staring at him.

"Please," said Harry, "I've brought Uncle Artie's fags."

There was a great roar of laughter. Somebody said, "Trust bloody Artie. He's got his own civvy batman now. I wish I had somebody to run errands for me."

"That bloody Artie. If he fell in the river, he'd come up wi' a fish in both hands."

Then a door opened at the far end, and Artie came out with a thickset man, with three stripes on his arm.

"Shake hands wi' the sergeant, Harry," said Artie.

Harry held out his hand, and tried hard to look the sergeant in the eye. The sergeant had close-cropped ginger hair, a ginger moustache, and terrible, piercing blue eyes that seemed to look right through Harry's soul.

"An' what are you on, lad?" said the sergeant, in a very booming voice.

"Please, sir, Artie's fags."

"You don't call me sir. You call me sarge."

The whole barrack fell about laughing, as if that was a very funny joke.

"There's only one man you call *sir*," said the sergeant. "And he doesn't look much bigger than you, or much older, an' he's got a little pip on his shoulder, and a little stick in his hand, that he keeps on dropping. But you needn't worry about him, cos he never comes down here except when he has to, cos he might get his lily-white hands dirty if he did."

The whole barrack fell about laughing again.

"So you run errands, boy?"

"Yes, sir… sarge."

"Will you run one for me?"

"Yes… sir… sarge."

"Well. You can run down to Amble – Huxtable's shop – and tell the lady behind the counter that I shall be a little late for tea, because my commanding officer has just given me a lot of silly little forms to fill in, about how many German planes we haven't shot down, and how many of this idle lot have got a dose of the crabs."

Everybody fell about laughing a third time, banging plates on tables, cheering and booing.

"An' here's sixpence for going." A huge red hand pressed into Harry's.

He was *in*.

He went back to the pillbox late that night. It was getting dark, and it felt silent and lonely after the barrack room. But he was full to bursting with beef stew and dumplings, and huge chunks of chocolate sponge pudding, drowned in thin watery custard. And so was Don.

And his head was bursting with all the new friends he'd made, and all the things he'd learnt. He'd learnt how to blanco a belt, and how to polish boot toe-caps by spitting on them, and how to polish the buckles on a soldier's belt without getting Brasso on the webbing. He'd even done some spelling for a man writing home to his wife. And he'd played football with a ball that sagged like a squashed melon, and been tossed up among the rafters of the barrack by a Scotsman, not a word of whose sayings he had understood.

Artie had seen him as far as the barbed wire.

"Enjoyed yerself?"

"Yeah."

"They're not a bad lot. They've nearly all got kids at home your age. They get bored. You're a new face, a bit of interest. You want to come an' see us again?"

"Yeah!"

"Come any time. Out o' working hours. There's just one feller you'll have to watch out for. Our snidey friend Corporal Merman… spiteful bugger, nobody likes him."

"Which one was he?" Harry couldn't think of anybody he hadn't liked, even the Scotsman.

"'Saright. He's on leave at the moment. For a fortnight, thank God. That's why everybody was so happy."

"What's the matter with him?"

"Oh… he's very regimental… wants another stripe… carries little tales to the officers… Oh, I don't know, all sorts of things. Whey-faced thin bugger, wi' spectacles. You'll soon spot him, when you see him."

"Goodnight, Uncle Artie."

"Goodnight, Harry. Mind how you go. Hope your mum's not worried…"

"She doesn't mind what I get up to."

"She should. I would if you were mine…"

"Tara, Uncle Artie." Harry had stumbled away, suddenly hardly able to look where he was going, for tears. He kept his head turned away, so Artie couldn't see them.

Now there was just the empty pillbox, and old memories. How could he be so miserable, after such a happy day?

But he cleaned out the grate, and broke up driftwood, and got a fire going, and piled on some of his hard-won sea-coal. As the fire roared up, and Don came to lie beside him and enjoy it, and the wind sighed outside, he suddenly felt better. Snug. This was nice, too, the sound of the wind and the sea, the soft patches of fur behind the dog's ears.

How could life be so good and yet so bad? You just thought things were great, and then life smashed them up. You'd just made up your mind things were bad, and then something good like this happened… it was just too hard to understand.

After a while, he slept.

He became a great favourite, and so did Don. They stuffed

him so full of bread and jam, great hunks of cheese and soldiers' biscuits that his belt began to get tight. They gave him a forage-cap with a badge, so he felt a real soldier. They gave him the smallest pair of old boots they could find, because the salt water of the beach was ruining his shoes. They showed him how to darn his socks, when they got holes in. They gave him spare socks, and the thing he valued most, a large pack with straps, that he could carry on his shoulders.

During the day, while they thought he should be at school, he still combed the beach. He didn't worry about food now, but he collected a vast amount of wood and sea-coal, so he could have a roaring fire every night. He found two old pans, to heat water in, and a battered enamel basin. He found a fresh stream running down the cliffs to the south, and filled a lot of bottles with drinking water. And he kept himself scrupulously clean, washing his shirt and vest and pants. Nobody wanted a dirty kid.

The worst thing he had to do was lie. They asked about his mam and his dad and his sister, and in an eerie way, his whole family came back to life. Only now they were in the cottage down the coast, and doing new things. He spent the walk to the camp making up new things that they did.

The best thing he did was the walks with Uncle Artie. Artie had been born in the country. Though he'd lived in

London since he was fifteen, he was still a country boy at heart. He liked to set snares for rabbits, which made a nice change from the army grub, cooked with potatoes over the barrack stove at night. He gave Harry the odd rabbit "for his mam". Harry cooked it over his own nightly fire. He learnt to set snares as well. He knew in his heart that Artie and the barracks were not forever. Some time he would be on his own again. He must be ready for it, though he came to dread it. It would happen, some day. Nothing good ever lasted.

But at least nobody came near the pillbox. Until one night, when he was lying by the fire on his blankets, giving the rabbit in the pan an occasional stir. When he felt safest, it happened.

Voices in the windy dark. He heard the woman's voice first, because it was shriller. The woman's voice was sharp, angry.

Then the rumble of a man's voice. They were quarrelling. He tensed up, waiting for them to pass. But they didn't. They stood quarrelling outside the pillbox.

"I'm not having any more of it," said the woman. "It's not fair to me, and it's not fair to your wife. I thought it was over, when you went away. I hated that, but I got used to it. And now you've come back, and you want to start all over again." It was very much a posh voice, a lady's voice.

The man rumbled something inaudible.

"Look," said the woman. "I know where you've been.

You've been over France. On those 'offensive fighter sweeps'. Every time I heard that our fighters had made an offensive sweep, and that only two of our aircraft failed to return, I thought one of them was you. I wrote you off; I made up my mind you were dead. Because you didn't write."

"You asked me not to write. You said it was over."

"Don't you understand how I *felt*?"

Rumble.

"All I had left were those poems you wrote me… what good are *poems*? Poems don't keep you warm."

"Look, let's get in here, out of the wind. I know you don't want to do anything, but we might as well get out of the wind."

And the next second, they were through the door, standing in the light of his fire, watching him. A tall man in RAF blue, and a slim beautiful girl with long dark hair.

Don gave a warning growl. Harry grabbed Don's collar. And still there was silence. Then the man said, quite gently, to Harry, "Who are *you*?" His voice was posh as well.

"Harry Baguley. I live here." He said it angrily, bitterly. All his safety was gone.

The pair of them looked about the pillbox; at the fire, the candle burning in its bottle, the blankets, the attaché case and large pack, the heap of sea-coal and the ragged rusty shovel he used to put it on the fire with. His home.

"You… live… here?" said the man. He sounded dumbfounded. "Where are your *parents*?"

"Killed. In the bombing."

"Where?"

"North Shields."

"When was that?"

"'Bout a month ago."

"And you're all alone?"

"I got the dog."

As if he understood, the dog growled softly, under his breath.

The man looked about. Then he said, "Do you mind if we sit down?"

They sat, the girl's beautiful silk-stockinged legs folded gracefully under her, the man's arm round her slim shoulders.

"Don't you mind, being on your own?" asked the girl.

"If they catch me, they'll…"

"Put you in a home?" The girl finished the sentence. Then she said, "But you want to be free?"

Harry nodded. It summed up his feelings as much as anything could.

"You poor little beggar," said the man kindly. But Harry flared up.

"I'm not a beggar. I got me dog. I got me friends. I

got me home." He glared round the pillbox angrily. "Now I suppose you're going to tell the police about me?"

"I wouldn't dream of it, old lad," said the man. "But what will you do when winter comes?"

"What does that matter?" said Harry. "It's summer now. I might be dead afore winter. So might you. I like it here *now*."

"Out of the mouths of babes and sucklings," said the girl. Then she added, "I think I like it here now too." She looked at the man with a new expression on her face. "We might *all* be dead tomorrow." She took his hand. His face strangely lit up.

"Look, old lad," said the man. "We couldn't borrow this… your place… for half an hour, could we? I'd take it as a great favour. You couldn't take your dog for a last walk along the beach? I always took my dog for a walk, last thing, when I was a boy."

Harry looked at them, holding hands. Suddenly he quite liked them. For some reason, he felt sorry for them. He wanted to look after them.

"OK," he said. "Bargain. You don't split on me to the police, and I'll take the dog for a walk along the beach. But how do I know when half an hour's up?"

"Borrow my watch," said the man. "It's got luminous hands." He slipped it off and gave it to Harry.

"Don't let the rabbit burn," said Harry. "Put more water in from that bottle." And then he and the dog were out in the whirling dark, with sheets of sand blowing along the beach, and stinging up into their faces.

He walked nearly to Joseph's cabin, then back. That gave them more time than they'd asked for.

When he got back, they were gone. But the fire was made up nicely, and the rabbit still cooking, and they had written, with the end of a burnt stick on the concrete floor,

Thank you, Harry Baguley.

Harry thought with a start that the man had forgotten his watch, his superb fighter pilot's watch.

But they never came back.

Chapter Ten

It was evening again. They were sitting on the cliffs,
watching the sea. Harry and Artie. So close they were
touching. That was Harry's doing; he liked to lean gently
against Artie, as if it was an accident.

The sea was up, crashing on the beach below. The sea
was blue as the sky, but when the waves reared up before
they broke, they went dark blue, then green, then creamy
white. There were birds flying along the troughs of the
waves, only feet above the water, shining as white as stars in
the light of the setting sun. Artie raised the binoculars. He
said the binoculars really belonged to the officer, but the
sergeant took care of them for the officer, and had loaned
them to Artie as a special favour.

"Just gulls," said Artie, in mild disgust. "Lesser black-backs." He handed the binoculars to Harry, who had a look just the same. It made him feel important, handling the binoculars, which had WD stamped on them.

Artie knew all about birds; and foxes and stoats and weasels. Artie knew all about the land, and Harry knew all about the sea, from Joseph. They told each other things; fair exchange no robbery.

"We mustn't be late," said Artie. "I've got me kit to do. And we don't want your mam worryin'."

Harry wriggled uncomfortably. That was the one worrying thing about Artie; he was always going on about Mam and Dad and Dulcie. As if he wanted to meet them, get to know them, be accepted by them. Harry hated lying, making excuses why Artie couldn't meet them. But what could you do?

"I shall come back here, after the war," said Artie. "Bring Dot and Keith for a holiday. You'd like our Keith. You'd get on well. He's a little monkey, just like you. God knows what you'd get up to together. D'you think you'll go on living here, after the war?"

"Dunno," said Harry, stamping down hard in his mind on this lovely impossible dream. "We haven't won the war yet. D'you think we're going to win?"

"I had me doubts in 1940. But now, with the Russians

and the Americans, yes, we'll win in the end. Muddle through, like we always do, I expect. I swear that's an eider duck with her ducklings, out there." He grabbed back the binoculars.

They watched the duck land through the breakers; Harry was terrified for the ducklings. They were so small, and the waves were so big and rough. The last duckling was too slow, was pulled back to sea by the undertow three times, struggling frantically, while the duck heedlessly walked away with the rest up the beach. Harry's heart was in his mouth. He knew how helpless and desperate the duckling must feel. As he watched it struggle, he *was* the duckling. At last it escaped the tugging waves with a final terrible effort, and scooted after the rest of the family. When, at last, it rejoined them, Harry heard Artie give out his breath with an explosive sigh.

"Bad mothers, eider ducks. They lose a lot of chicks doing that kind of thing. Nature's very cruel."

"Aye," said Harry.

"Bloody Corporal Merman comes back from leave tomorrow," said Artie. "You'll have to watch it at the barracks. Try not to get across him. Miserable sod. I don't know why God makes people like that. A misery to himself and others."

Harry felt his stomach squeeze tight. It had been such a

great fortnight. All the fun in the barrack room. The lads shouting for him.

"Where's that young Harry?", "Haaarry... Haarry! Nip down the NAAFI for me, kid, will you? Twenty Capstan Full-Strength and a quarter of mint humbugs?", "Our Harry's a-going to be a soldier, when he grows up, in the Ar-tiller-ey!"

Even the sergeant had rolled in one night, mildly drunk from the sergeant's mess at the airfield, and put Harry through his drill with comic gusto.

"Stannart ease... tenshun... left turn, left turn, right turn, about turn... wait for it, *wait* for it!"

He belonged; belonged to everybody. But there was no one like Artie, the walks alone with Artie.

"Hey," said Artie with a squeak. "Gannets!" Again he grabbed the binoculars off Harry's lap, and turned the focusing-wheel rapidly. "Yes, yes. Just out beyond that red marker-buoy down the coast. They're *diving*; diving for fish." Artie had leapt to his feet, and Harry with him. "Here, look!"

Harry twiddled the focus-wheel. Got a brief close-up of old Joseph's cabin, with the chimney smoking, then swivelled out to sea. Just in time to see a huge white yellow-tipped gannet fold its wings and fall like a Stuka dive-bomber. It hit the water like a dart, vanished with hardly a ripple, and then the sea boiled and the gannet was struggling back into the air with gangling, waterladen, furiously beating wings.

And another. And another. "Cor," said Harry, and moved outwards for a better view. He heard Artie shout a warning, and at the same moment, the grass and soil under his left foot gave way. He dropped the glasses, saw Artie's outstretched hand and grabbed for it, touched it but couldn't get a grip, and the next minute he was falling, falling.

Something hit him a terrible blow on the back of the neck, a pain shot up his left leg, then he was staring up at Artie's tiny head peering down, far above, on the cliff top.

"Don't *move*," shouted Artie. "I'm coming down."

He just lay and watched Artie placing his hobnailed boots ever so carefully, as he came down the cliff.

"Anything broken?" asked Artie, touching him anxiously all over.

"Gotta headache." Harry raised both his arms and waggled them. Then he waggled his legs. Everything seemed to be all right.

"How many fingers am I holding up?" asked Artie.

"One, stupid." Harry giggled with relief.

"D'you think you can try to stand?" Artie helped him to his feet.

"Fine," said Harry. Then tried to take a step forward with his left leg. As he put the weight on the foot, he shouted, "Ouch."

"What is it? Your ankle?"

"Be all right in a minute," gasped Harry, gritting his teeth, and taking three more steps. "It'll wear off." But it didn't.

"You've either sprained your ankle or broken it. I'd better get you home, and your mam can call the doctor…"

"No… no," said Harry.

"What you mean, no, no? I can carry you easy. You're no weight at all. I'll give you a piggy-back. Just tell me where to go." Artie picked up the fallen binoculars, gave them a quick once-over, and hung them round his neck. "I'll go along the beach to that low place where there's a path. The dog'll follow us along the cliff." He slung Harry on his back as easy as if he was a sack of potatoes.

And so they went, the smell of Artie's hair in Harry's nostrils, the smell of tobacco and sweat, the best most homely smell in the world. Except they were going to…

"There's our cottage," said Harry, as the pillbox came in sight. "I can walk from here," he added miserably. "Put me down."

"Not on your nelly, son," said Artie. "I'll see you safe home with your mam, and tell her what's happened…" His head was down, with the effort of carrying Harry. He didn't see the "cottage" fall apart bit by bit, as they got nearer; the slates off the roof, the peeling painted brickwork that Harry saw.

"We're here," said Harry bitterly. Artie put him down and looked up.

"A bloody pillbox! Is this your idea of a joke? Stop mucking about, Harry lad. It's getting late."

"This is where I live."

"With yer mam and dad?"

"I haven't got any mam and dad."

"Well, this beats all," said Artie, sitting back on his heels and scratching his head. "You're a good plucked 'un," he added, surveying the swept floor, the big pile of dry sea-coal and wood, the heap of newspapers and the row of bottles of water. "What you sleep on?"

"My stuff's hidden in the roof. Can you get it down for me?"

When Artie had got it, he said admiringly, "You'd make a bloody good spy. You've got everything to your convenience here."

"I manage."

Artie's eyes flared in alarm. "Aye, but you can't manage now. That ankle could be broken. You could be suffering from concussion. You should be seen to by a doctor, mebbe in the hospital."

"If you split on me, it's the end of everything. They'll take Don away…"

Artie looked quite demented. "You don't know what you're asking of me, son! I might come back in the morning an' find you dead."

Harry said wildly, "I'd rather be dead than in a hospital."

"Don't talk so wet."

"Look, Artie, give me one chance. If my ankle's no better by tomorrow morning, you can fetch the doctor…"

They looked at each other a long, long time.

Then Artie said at last, "Till the morning then. I'll do up your ankle wi' a tight wet bandage Keep it wet from the bottles. Lucky I always carry two clean hankies. You've got nowt here that would do. By God, that ankle's swelling up like a football… I'll not sleep a wink tonight, worrying about you…"

He was as good as his word. He was back by dawn, with a flask of hot tea and plenty of bully-beef sandwiches. He prodded the ankle doubtfully. "It's gone down a bit. I think. Doesn't feel so hot. Try walking on it."

Harry walked. He had to clench his teeth, and sweat broke out on his forehead, but he walked. He would have walked if it had killed him.

"Ye've been lucky," said Artie. "I think it's just a sprain.

I'll tie it up tight again, and you don't move a muscle, right? I'll be back to bring you your supper after work."

For four nights, and days, Harry obediently lay still. Mostly he slept; the rest of the time he crawled out into the sunshine and watched the beach and the sea. He felt oddly relaxed. It was like having a real dad looking after you. By the fourth night, he could walk quite well again. He said, "I'll be up to see you at camp tomorrow."

"The lads have been wondering where you've got to. They'll be pleased to see you back. It's just as well you've mended. That bloody Merman's been wondering what I've been up to, dashing out of camp at all hours like that... nosy sod..."

Chapter Eleven

The next evening, up at the camp, Harry had his first sight
of Corporal Merman. Corporal Merman was sitting on his
bed, opposite Artie's. The sergeant slept in a little room at
one end of the barrack called a "bunk" and the two
corporals slept at the other end, to keep order. If anyone
could be said to keep order.

But Artie had been right. Corporal Merman did make a
difference to the barrack room. Nobody was dancing on
their bed in their shirt-tails tonight. They were all just sitting
talking, almost muttering. Most of them with their backs to
Corporal Merman.

He was a tall thin man, with blond newly washed hair,
and a mouth as prim as a spinster's. His battledress trousers

seemed to be made of a finer, thinner material than anybody else's, and they had creases like knives. There was an ironing board in the space by his bed, and newly ironed shirts hung on hangers everywhere. Even his white braces seemed cleaner and neater than the other men's. His face was long and very pale, shiny, almost as if it was a waxwork. He was polishing an already immaculate boot, but you could tell his large ears were busy listening.

There were a few shouts of welcome for Harry, but they were a bit half-hearted.

"Here's my favourite boy!"

"Nip down to the NAAFI for me, Harry?"

"What's this boy doing here?" asked Corporal Merman. "This is a military establishment – civilians aren't allowed." His voice seemed thin and weak, but it carried. There was a silence. Then there were low boos and jeers from all the way up the barrack room, an angry sound.

"Stuff it, Merman," said Artie. "The kid does no harm. He goes to the NAAFI for us."

"And a *dog*," said Corporal Merman. "That's against King's Regulations. Does the sergeant know about this, *Corporal* Blenkinsop?"

"He does, as a matter of fact, *Corporal* Merman." The bunk door had opened silently, and the massive figure of the sergeant stood there, his braces hanging round his legs, and a towel round his neck. "This dog – and this kid – are battery mascots. And very popular, unlike *some* I could mention, Corporal Merman."

Corporal Merman swallowed and smiled a thin cold smile, as if he'd swallowed an acid-drop whole.

The sergeant turned to Harry. "Nip down to the NAAFI for me, kid. An ounce of Player's Uncut."

Harry took everybody's order, and left. When he got back, the atmosphere in the hut didn't seem any better. He gave out the things and change, but all the time he felt Merman's cold eyes watching him. How could one man destroy the fun for so many? He didn't want to stay tonight. He wished Artie would ask him to go for a walk. But Artie was oddly quiet.

In the end, the incoherent Scotsman suggested a game of football. Everybody played rougher than usual, and even Harry got one or two nasty kicks, though he was sure they weren't meant. Merman kept watching out of the open window by his bed, with a superior sneer on his face.

Finally, he yelled at Harry, "Boy, boy come here!" Harry tried to ignore him as long as possible; but he wouldn't be ignored. The game stopped; another silence fell. With everybody watching, Harry walked across to the window.

"I want you to go to the NAAFI for me, boy. I need a tube of toothpaste…"

"He only goes down to the NAAFI once. Once every night," somebody shouted.

"Leave the kid alone," shouted somebody else.

"He doesn't *really* need toothpaste."

"Just trying to spoil the kid's game of football."

"Well, will you go or won't you?" asked Merman. He looked at Harry with pale, pale blue eyes. They reminded him of the eyes of a wolf he'd once seen at Edinburgh Zoo. He felt that if he went the errand for Merman, he'd somehow be in Merman's *power*. And that was the very last thing he wanted. He never wanted to go near Merman ever again. Merman made him want to shiver.

"Gotta get home to me mam," said Harry, and walked away.

"I'll remember that," said Merman.

"Goodnight, kid," shouted the football players. And went back to kicking the deflated ball about, miserably.

The next day was Saturday. Harry went across to the barrack in the afternoon. As he approached the door, it seemed unusually quiet. But he walked in anyway, and then he wished he hadn't.

There was nobody there. Except Corporal Merman, sitting on his bunk.

"Where's everybody?" Harry faltered.

"Your friend Corporal Blenkinsop had to march them down to the airfield for a shower. It was his turn."

"What about you?"

"Oh, I've had my shower. I have a shower every day, if I can. What do they say? Cleanliness is next to godliness?"

"Tell them I'll come back later."

"No, no, they've been gone over an hour. They'll be back any minute. Come and sit by me, boy." He patted the bed beside him. "I'm expecting them back any minute."

Harry hesitated. One part of him was yelling at him not to go near Merman at any cost. But another part... it was creepy... wanted to make friends with Merman, get Merman on his side, so he didn't have to be afraid of him any more.

"I've got a Mars Bar here," said Merman. "Like to share it with me? I know all you boys love Mars Bars..."

That decided Harry, against his better judgement. He could never resist a gesture of friendship. Maybe the awful Corporal Merman was human after all.

He sat down. Corporal Merman got the Mars Bar out of his bedside locker, put it on top, unwrapped it neatly, without tearing the wrapping paper, just folding it back like a bedsheet. Then he got out his very sharp shiny clasp-knife and cut it in nine thin slices, like a loaf of bread.

He picked up the first piece, precisely, between finger

and thumb, and held it up to Harry's mouth. Feeding him like a baby. Harry did not want to open his mouth, but he had to. He did not like the feel of Merman's fingertips on his lips.

"You're a big strong lad," said Merman. "You're very *brown*. I'll bet you have lots of girlfriends… no? Not any? Not ever? I would've thought you'd have had a girlfriend by your age. Aren't girls nice to *squeeze*?" He put an arm round Harry's waist, found a fold of skin and nipped it very playfully.

Harry wriggled violently, and Merman let go and fed him another piece of Mars Bar.

"I'll bet you have fun with that dog of yours though. Running about the beach, wrestling in the sand…"

Harry had a very nasty idea that Merman had been spying on him, when he hadn't realised Merman was there.

"And of course you're a great *friend* of Corporal Blenkinsop's. You spend a lot of time together, don't you? Walks in the woods and along the cliffs…"

"We do nature study," shouted Harry, suddenly furious, for no reason he could quite work out. "We watch birds an'… foxes."

"Yes, of course. Nature study, of course. You must take me to see all these birds and foxes, some evening…" He fed Harry a third bit of Mars Bar, holding it so high that he forced Harry's head back. "And... you do other things with Corporal Blenkinsop..."

"Like *what*?" Harry wondered why he was getting so angry and flustered. "We watched gannets," he added lamely, after a silence.

"Of course. Gannets..."

Just then, there was the crunch of boots on the road outside. Boots approaching at a trot, not a walk.

"Hup two three, hup two three," came Artie's urgent voice.

Harry took a quick peep at Merman's face.

The look on Merman's face was indescribable.

All the men came barging into the barrack room, hitting each other with wet towels again.

"Hello, *Corporal* Merman. Fancy finding you here." Artie's eyes took in, in one glance, the two of them sitting on the bed, the sliced Mars Bar. "Coming for a walk, Harry?"

Harry came like a flash. As they left, Artie shouted back at Merman, "If they ever catch you at it, Merman, they won't just take away your two little stripes. They'll put you away in Colchester for five bloody years."

They walked along the road. The silence was heavy, like the dark grey sky.

"I don't like him," said Harry timidly.

"Quite right, son. Never go near him. When I realised what he might be up to, I couldn't get the lads back quick enough. They did the whole return journey at the double, just for you. I hope you're honoured."

"What is he up to?"

"Never you mind, son. I wouldn't foul up your mind by telling you. Just stay away from him, *right*?"

"Right."

But nothing did seem to go right, that afternoon. Harry could tell that Artie was very very angry, and that seemed to frighten all the birds and animals away.

Chapter Twelve

Harry wakened on Sunday morning, feeling blackly miserable. It wasn't just that it was pouring with rain outside, though that didn't help. He just felt all wrong, jangled, jumbled up inside, and he couldn't tell what was wrong at all.

Except it was about Merman. He could think of nothing but Merman. He tried to think about Artie, or the incoherent Scotsman, or the man who danced on the end of his bed; but whatever he tried to think about, Merman kept sliding back into his mind. What did Merman *want*? He was like nobody Harry had ever met before. He was used to kind people, like Artie. He was used to brutal people, like the farmer with the shotgun. He had even met one or two people who were a bit nutty, like Joseph. And selfish people, who didn't give two damns about you.

But Merman wasn't any of those. Merman wanted something off him, and he just didn't know what. It made him feel very unsafe. So unsafe and miserable that he just got the fire going, munched a miserable bit of breakfast, and lay on, snug and warm inside his blankets. He cuddled Don a bit and then Don got tired and mooched off for a walk.

He heard footsteps coming along the path. Leapt up, cursing himself for a careless idiot. The person passing would notice the smoke from the chimney and come and look in. After all his carefulness, his hiding place was discovered.

Then he recognised the scrunch of hobnailed boots. A soldier. It must be Artie, come to see what was the matter with him. Artie would listen to him, explain the odd way he felt. Artie would make things better.

He looked up with an attempt at a grin, as the doorway darkened.

But it wasn't Artie. It was Corporal Merman.

"There you are," said Merman. "Snug in your little nest."

Harry couldn't think of anything to say to that. He just screwed up in a ball, inside his blankets, and stared at Merman, trying to read his face in the half-light. Merman was smiling; it wasn't a very nice smile. It was a sort of smirky triumphant smile, pretending to be friendly.

"Very comfy you've made yourself. You and Corporal Blenkinsop." Merman came and sat down close to him, as he had the other time. There was nothing that Harry could do about it. Merman was between him and the door.

"I'll bet you have a lot of fun in here," said Merman. "With your *nature studies*." He sort of sniggered to himself.

"We don't come in here much," said Harry. "We go for walks."

"Well, I don't suppose Corporal Blenkinsop minds where you go. As long as you're *kind* to him."

Harry thought that was a very strange thing to say. You weren't *kind* to adults. You liked them. Or obeyed them. You weren't *kind* to them.

"We're mates," he said at last.

"Of course you are," said Merman. "Just as you and I are going to be *mates*." He put a cold damp hand on Harry's bare arm. It was horrible, like touching a dead fish.

"I choose my own mates," said Harry, pulling his arm away. He blurted it out, and then wished he hadn't. He didn't want to get Merman angry; he thought he might turn nasty. But he couldn't stand Merman hovering over him like that; touching him.

"Choosy, are we?" said Merman. He didn't seem annoyed; more excited. "I wouldn't get too choosy if I was you. Or you and your mate Corporal Blenkinsop might end up in a great deal of trouble with the police. Corporal Blenkinsop might end up going to *prison*."

"What we *done*?" squeaked Harry. His mind flew across all the things he had done. Lying to the chip-shop man, hitting the farmer, eating army grub. Not having a licence for Don. How could they send Artie to prison for things like *that*?

"But that doesn't have to happen," said Corporal Merman. "Not if you're as *kind* to me as you have been to Corporal Blenkinsop." He took hold of Harry's arm and squeezed it again. A painful nip.

Harry went berserk. He pulled his arm away, and tried to kick out at Merman. But the blankets hindered him, and Merman just edged out of the way, laughing. But it did knock the blankets wide, exposing Harry's legs and underpants. And Harry caught Merman's eyes drifting down to his underpants, and he pulled the blankets back round himself, desperately. He'd suddenly got Merman's number. Merman was like the dirty boys at school. The ones who hung around the toilets and messed about with you when you went for a pee. Poking you in the back while you were busy, and making you pee all over your shoes. Or making remarks about you, or trying to grab your balls, which hurt like hell. Only they never went very far in the toilets, because there might always be somebody else coming in, who might run and tell tales to the teacher.

He was alone with Merman. Well, nearly alone. Suddenly he was yelling for Don, at the top of his voice.

"That won't do you any good," said Merman. "You haven't got a licence for that dog, have you? If I tell the police, they'll come and take your dog away. I don't think he's really your dog anyway... I think he's a stray. Or you stole him..."

Harry heard Don bark on the beach. Getting nearer. Then silence. No sound of paws. No more barks. No Don. Hope died.

"Your dog's not coming," said Merman. "He's got better things to do. Perhaps he's found a bitch on heat..." Again, that smirk. Again, his hand reaching for Harry's arm.

"C'mon," Merman wheedled. "You've only got to be nice to me. It won't take long. I can bring you things. Sweets. Mars Bars. Things for your dog..."

"I don't know what you mean," shouted Harry.

Then the doorway darkened again. Don was standing there. Don was growling, a deep rumble that was half-choked.

Because a hand was hooked tight round Don's collar.

Artie's hand.

Artie didn't look at Harry. He avoided Harry's look. He

said to Merman, "Come outside, you filthy bastard. I'm going to give you a hiding you won't forget to your dying day." Harry could hardly recognise it was Artie. Artie looked hardly human.

Merman tried to bluster. Merman's voice shook, but he tried to sound reasonable.

"I'm not wanting anything you haven't done," he said. "You sneaking along to this kid, morning and night. I saw you. I followed you here. You're crazy for the kid. You couldn't get enough of him."

"Come out," said Artie in a dreadful voice. "Come out or I'll let this dog loose on you. And then I'll *drag* you out and deal with what the dog's left…"

"No need to take it that way. We've both seen plenty of it in the Army…"

"Plenty of what?" Artie turned to Harry. "Have I ever touched you, Harry?"

"Only to bandage me leg," said Harry. He turned to Merman. "I sprained my ankle. He was looking after me."

Something seemed to flicker out and die in Merman's eyes. Leaving him looking pale and ill.

"All right, I was wrong," he said to Artie. "How was I to know? Be reasonable…"

Harry felt a tiny flicker of sympathy for him; only a tiny flicker. Because he looked so… lost.

The next second, Artie had let go of the dog and grabbed Merman, and was dragging him on his knees out of the pillbox. The dog was barking wildly, and Artie was swearing like a man possessed.

Harry was still trying to quieten Don when he heard the first blows. Harry didn't try to follow. He just sat listening to the sounds of the fighting and Artie swearing, and remembering the lost look on Merman's face.

Then he heard Merman screaming and sobbing. "Stop it, stop it, stop it." Terror drove him out of the pillbox. To see Merman on the ground, and Artie with a boot raised.

"Stop it, Artie. You'll *kill* him!"

There was a trickle of blood down Artie's face from a cut lip. But Merman was writhing on the ground with his hands over his face, and his hands were red with blood. Harry flung himself at Artie; grabbed him round the legs shouting, "Stop it, stop it."

At last, Artie relaxed, and stood still, just panting and slobbering. Then he licked the cut on his mouth, and drew a hand across his face. And looked down at Harry, and said, "Hullo, kid. It's you." His face still looked very strange.

"You coulda *killed* him," said Harry.

Artie sat down heavily on the grass. "Aye, mebbe you're right. I wouldn't want to swing for that bugger – he's not worth it." He was still taking deep shuddering breaths.

"Merman didn't hurt me, honest! He was just pestering me."

"I know, lad. I followed him from the camp, the dirty bastard. Saw him going along the cliff. Nobody walks along the cliffs this weather. So I knew he was coming after you. I knew he'd spotted your hiding place. He must have seen me coming here, when you were poorly wi' your leg…"

"You mean – all the time he was talking to me, you were *listening*?"

"Aye. I had to make sure what he was up to, the dirty bastard. Had to wait for him to show his hand. That's why I hung on to your dog, when you called him. I had to hear what he was sayin' to you…"

"WHY?"

"Because he was *jealous*!" It was a new creaky voice. They both turned and stared. Merman had hauled himself to his feet. His face was hideous, a mask of brown drying blood. "He was jealous. Because he wants the same thing from you as me. Only he was scared to ask for it."

"You filthy bastard." Artie leapt to his feet and made for Merman again. But Harry clung to Artie's legs, and tripped Artie up, so he fell full length. And Merman went staggering off along the cliff top, like a drunken scarecrow. When he was at a safe distance, he turned and shouted, "I'll get you for this. Both of you."

Then he staggered away out of sight.

They sat on a long time, staring at the sea, Artie dabbing at his cut mouth with a clean white handkerchief that slowly turned into a bouquet of bloodstains, getting fainter and fainter.

Finally, Artie said, "I'd never have touched you, Harry. You know that. Not like he thought. It's just his twisted mind. He thinks everybody is like he is."

"I know," said Harry miserably. "You're a married man with a son my age."

"That doesn't mean much," said Artie bitterly. "So is he. I feel sorry for his wife." Then he shrugged, and said, "We're sitting here like a couple of loonies, getting ourselves soaked. Let's get out of the weather."

They went back into the pillbox, and Harry made up the fire. They tried to get the bloodspots out of Artie's battledress jacket, but they wouldn't come out.

"Will you get in trouble?" asked Harry.

"What? A corporal having a fight wi' a corporal? Happens all the time, in this man's army. It'll cost me for a new battledress, that's all. 'Less I can scrounge one from the quartermaster. But it's the end of a perfect friendship, our Harry. You can't stay here. He can make trouble for *you*."

"Why? What've I done?"

"Sleeping rough. Stealing a dog. You've got to move on,

son. He'll probably be on the phone to the police, the moment he gets himself cleaned up. Anonymous phone call, of course. No names, no pack-drill. Look, you get packed up and get to that road over yonder. I'll walk back to camp an' borrow a thirty-hundredweight and set you on your road. Where were you goin', when we first met?"

"Holy Island. Lindisfarne."

"Right. Lindisfarne it is. Unless the tide's in."

But the tide was in. Lindisfarne was an island, cut off by a mile of sea, almost hidden, a grey long flat shadow in the teeming rain.

"I've got to get back to camp," said Artie. "I'm on guard duty in an hour, and me kit's filthy. But I can't leave you out in this…"

He sat with his hands clenched round the steering wheel, chewing at his teeth, the lines deepening on his face. Harry knew he was in agony; like a fox caught by its leg in a trap, and the trap was the Army. If Artie wasn't on duty in an hour, he'd be in real trouble; lose his stripes, maybe get sent to the glasshouse.

He must let Artie out of the trap; it was the one good thing to do, though it felt like stepping off the edge of the world.

He said, gently, trying to keep the tremor out of his

voice, "Find me a thick hawthorn hedge. Under a tree. That'll keep me dry."

Artie looked at him; his eyes were grateful and very ashamed. "Ye're a good kid. I wish I could take you home to my missus. She'd look after you. This bloody awful war…"

They had to drive around quite a lot, to find a hawthorn hedge with a tree. But they found one at last, and Artie lifted down all his kit, gave Don a last rough desperate pat, shook hands and drove away without looking back. It was only after the truck had vanished that Harry realised he had something pressed into his right hand, after Artie's last handshake. A little wad of dirty paper. He opened it up, and saw three very oily pound notes. And heard again Artie's last desperate words.

"Keep in touch, son. Let me know you're getting on all right."

Three pounds. That was a whole week's wages for Artie. More. How would he afford his fags now? And Harry didn't even need the money. He had plenty of *money*. When he got settled again, he would write to Artie, and send the money back.

Meanwhile, he was getting wet. With no means of getting dry again. That was the only thing that made sense at the moment.

Harry forced his way into the hedge. It was quite dry in there; lots of dry leaf-mould, with only a few prickles.

He curled up tight with Don, smelling the doggy smell of him for comfort, driving his face into Don's fur, to block the world out. And he slept; a queer jerky sleep full of dreams that switched from one scene to another. Sometimes he was sea-coaling on the beach with Joseph; sometimes walking through the woods with Artie; sometimes back at his own house, staring at the little blue flames licking up from the bricks that had once been home; and sometimes on the beach before the war, building sandcastles. But always, Merman was somewhere about, Merman with his bleeding face, wanting...

Then he would jolt awake, and see the dull grey sky showing through the dark green hawthorn leaves, and hear the endless sound of the rain, and know that Merman was far away. Like everything else. Everything was far away, except the world, which was a big black cold hole now, reaching in with icy fingers to steal his very life.

Then he would bury his face in Don's warm fur and sleep again.

It was the sunset that woke him, shining in through the leaves. A magnificent sunset. It had stopped raining, and the pilot's watch said four hours had passed. Six o'clock.

Above his head, the hedge and big tree were dripping. Right on to his head. They had kept him dry till now, but they were going to make him very wet, if he stayed much longer.

Nothing for it but to get on the move again. And he was ravenous.

He stumped along, head down, not wanting to look at the world. Don ran ahead, full of life, questing for food without a care in the world.

Once again, Harry wished he was a dog.

Chapter Thirteen

He walked up the rain-soaked road, towards the sunset, which was a lovely lemon-yellow, and turning the road lemon-yellow too, so he seemed to walk on the light, on sky. It lifted him a little; above the dense mass of misery about Artie. While the sunset lasted, he felt he could keep going, could almost *fly* above his troubles. But he knew that when the dark came, he'd plunge deep, deep back into them. Keep walking; keep walking away from them.

Around him, the fields were empty. But there was a house ahead, where the road met the sky. A house with two chimneys smoking. They must be rich, to have two fires going at once, in wartime. He imagined a table laid for supper, with cloth serviettes and heavy silver knives and forks, like they had in Carrick's Café, in Newcastle. Pork pie and chips – big fat Carrick's chips. The thought was a mistake – his belly filled up suddenly with the fizzy liquid of hunger. But he went on with his fantasy about the house. It was the house of somebody he knew – they were waiting for him to come home.

Oddly enough, at that point (and he was still a hundred yards away), the figure of a woman came out of the garden gate, and stood in the road, watching. Only she was in silhouette against the sunset, and he couldn't tell if she was staring at him or away from him. But he could tell from the way her elbows stuck out that her hands were clasped tight together. She was waiting for somebody, and anxious as well. He still had the absurd idea she was waiting for him; but it must be somebody out of sight, beyond the brow of the hill, for there was no one on the road behind him. He'd checked.

Then, as he got nearer, he saw she *was* looking at him; she had come down the road ten paces towards him. She gestured to him, as if urging him on.

Again he looked behind him; but there was nobody.

She shouted something urgent, which he couldn't make out. Unable to bear the suspense, he broke into a feeble trot, all the weight of the pack and pans on his back banging away.

As he neared her, she reached out and grabbed both his hands. He looked, bewildered, at her middle-aged bespectacled face. He didn't know her from Adam. She was a total stranger. But she was yelling at him urgently.

"My mother's fallen on the stairs, an' I can't lift her! Come quick and help me lift her!"

If she hadn't been holding his hands, he might well have run away. He was scared of old age and illness. He had enough troubles of his own. But the woman had a firm grip on him, so he went. Up the crazy-paving path, with huge white conch-shells lined up on both sides. Dreading what he might see, when his eyes got used to the dark hallway.

A massive bulk, at the foot of the stair. Fat grey-clad legs sprawled any old how, skirt right up above the knees. A clutter of sprawled arms and knobbly sticks. And a face.

The face smiled up at him. "There's a kind lad," the old lady said. It was a headmistressy sort of face, with white hair piled high, and gold-rimmed spectacles perched on the nose, and dangling a gold chain. He knew in an instant this was no useless old granny; this was somebody far too important to be left lying in a heap at the bottom of the stairs.

"If you'll take this hand," said the old lady, as calm and decisive as Field Marshal Montgomery, "Ada can manage the other. Now, both heave together. And stop *flapping*, Ada! I'm not dead yet."

There was one tremendous heave, and she was on her feet, her spectacles wildly awry. She adjusted them, and said, "Sticks!"

Ada grovelled behind her, and produced the sticks. The old lady settled her grip on them both, nodded to Harry, as if to say all was well, and said, "Come in, young man," and led the way in stately fashion.

The room was large and cosy, with a blazing fire and bookshelves all over the walls. But what caught his eye was a table laid for supper. With big fat silver knives and forks, just like at Carrick's Café.

"You'll stay for a bite, of course. Take his bags upstairs, Ada. And set another place. We must look after our rescuer. Do sit down, Master... I'm afraid I didn't catch your name?"

"Harry... Baguley." He shook hands solemnly.

"I expect you would like to wash your hands, Master Baguley? Show him the bathroom, Ada."

The bathroom smelt fragrant and female. Like their bathroom at home, after Mam had had a bath, only much more so. He was almost afraid to use the pale pink towel, in case he left a dirty mark on it. He washed his face and hands three times, then dried them on his filthy handkerchief. But he borrowed a large pink comb and combed his hair, and carefully checked for hairs afterwards, and pulled the hairs out of the comb and put them in his pocket to throw away later. Then he grew afraid he had made that small dirty mark on the pale pink carpet, and spent three minutes trying to scrub that out with his hanky and spit.

He hovered on the landing, suddenly terribly shy. But the old lady's head appeared, and she said, "Ah, there you are!" And then he *had* to go downstairs.

"Do sit here. I expect you're ready for your supper. I see you've been camping! You haven't had very good weather for the first week of your holiday!"

"No, it's been a bit wet." He realised how posh her voice was, against his own. Even though he was talking to her the proper way he talked to the teachers at school.

"Camping by the sea?" He followed her eyes. There was a small pile of sand on the carpet, where his bag had rested for a moment. His mouth fell open with embarrassment, but she just said, "I've loved the sea all my life, since I was a young gel. Used to swim every day – three times a day, when I could. My father used to call me the Mermaid."

He thought she didn't look much like a mermaid now. She said, "I don't look much like a mermaid now, do I?" and roared with laughter. Then she said, "Tell me all the things you've been up to. Your dog's quite snug in the kitchen, by the way. Ada found a ham bone for him, with a bit of meat on."

So he told her all about Joseph, while Ada bustled in with plates of sliced ham and tomato, and a stand full of scones, and a large sponge cake.

By the end of tea, his belt felt very tight. He knew he had made a pig of himself, but she kept on urging him on, with a kind of glee. "I know what appetites young men like you have." Half-way through tea, the sunset had faded, and it had begun to rain, a heavy hopeless rain that battered at the windows. When he had refused a fourth piece of cake, the old lady pushed back her chair, grasped her sticks and said, "Not a night for camping-out, I'm afraid. Come and sit by the fire." Then, when he had sat, she said, "Ada, make up the bed in young David's room."

And that was that. He might as well have been kidnapped and chained up, for all the chance he had of getting away that night. But he didn't seem to mind. He was full, he was warm and he had lost any desire to go anywhere. A great calm had descended on him.

Until Ada returned, and said, "What about pyjamas?"

"Lay out a pair of David's. I'm sure boys don't wear pyjamas when they're camping. And lay out David's dressing gown and slippers." She looked at Harry's startled face. "David won't mind. Much too busy hunting U-boats off Bermuda. And getting-off with the local girls, I have no doubt." She smiled conspiratorially, and he smiled back. She said, "It's nice having a boy around the house again. Though why nice boys turn into boring middle-aged men, I've no idea. Tell me about your school."

It was a long cosy evening. She was a good listener, and he talked more than he had done for years. About making a model yacht and sailing it, with Dad. About bullying at school. It was hard to keep off the things he didn't want her to know, the dark bits, the last bombing, the fight between Artie and Corporal Merman.

They hardly saw Ada at all. First she was washing up in the kitchen, then she was making up the bed upstairs. Then she was fetching supper drinks.

"That dog dry yet? Good. Boys always like to go to bed with their dogs. Just take him a walk round the garden first, Ada. It's stopped raining, and we don't want any doggy accidents, do we, Harry?"

Then she talked on, herself. About before the war, and the weekend parties, and the housefuls of young men, and the horses and sailing-boats, and sailing out to the Farnes and having picnics, with the gulls wheeling overhead, catching tit-bits on the wing. How fascinating she was! He'd never realised how fascinating an old person could be. Not like the dull middle-aged Ada, who seemed to do nothing but work and ask what was next to be done.

It was midnight before the party broke up. It was the grandfather clock striking twelve that did it.

"I must go to bed," she said, "like Cinderella."

He stood up, the spell broken.

"Give me a goodnight kiss, Harry," she said. "I might be sixty, but I still enjoy being kissed by handsome young men."

But it was the silent Ada who showed him up to his room, where the sheets were turned down, and the pyjamas laid out. Pyjamas that were far too big for him.

"Will you be all right... getting her upstairs?" asked Harry worriedly.

"She's better at going up," said Ada shortly. "Goodnight."

He had to roll the sleeves of the pyjamas up, or they'd have been unbearable. But he and Don slept soundly, with the scent of lavender sheets filling the room.

In the morning, Ada wakened him with a cup of tea.

"Breakfast'll be ready in half an hour."

The table was laid for one.

"Where's...?"

"In bed," said Ada shortly. "And will be, for the next three days. That's if she's lucky. She overdid things last night. She always does, when she has a man around the house. She always liked the men."

"I'm sorry…"

"Don't be sorry. You did her a lot of good really. She doesn't see much of life now."

"David… all the others?"

"Too busy with the war. We've not seen anybody but the postman for months. When they're not fighting, they're living it up in London. I don't blame them really. They need their relaxation. But they don't know how bad she is. And she'll not let me write and tell them. Proud, she is. She'll not have their pity. Not when she could always wrap them round her little finger, when she was younger. That's her, when she was young."

She showed him a photograph, from the mantelpiece, in a silver frame.

The young girl was laughing, eyes full of mischief. Wearing a white sailor-dress, and holding the hand of a man in blazer and white flannels. They looked very happy together.

"Is that… her husband?"

"No – just one of her young men. She had so many young men. They took her sailing… fox-hunting… up in airplanes later on. She was always one for a dare. She took part in the London-Paris air race when she was forty-four – climbed Mont Blanc when she was forty-eight. With young men half her age."

"What about you?"

"I was never one for that sort of thing. But you… Master Harry… you're the last of a long line."

"Can't I say goodbye?"

"She wouldn't like you seeing her… as she is now. Go on, eat your breakfast and get off. Wherever you're going."

She came to the gate, to see him off. With a pack of fresh-made sandwiches.

"Can I… come back again?"

"You can try. Don't leave it too long."

Chapter Fourteen

It was a grand morning. As he headed back towards the sea the sun shone in his eyes, and he felt zooms of excitement running through him; zooms he couldn't explain at all, except the grass was so green, and twinkling with last night's rain, and there were flowers everywhere in the grass, tiny spots of yellow and blue; and all the birds were singing their heads off, and he seemed to have it all to himself. The whole show was for his benefit. And the sandwiches put him one meal away from worry; today, he would not have to think about food, with that huge breakfast inside him that made even burping a pleasure, for it brought back the tastes of porridge and bacon and egg and marmalade.

He reached the coast in a rush, for the land sloped down

towards the sea. And there, spread before him, lay the island of Lindisfarne, with the road to it clear, a dark bar of sand leading across the shining water. Everything was on his side, and he made up his mind. To Lindisfarne he would go. He was a pilgrim, and he would finish his pilgrimage.

He was as ignorant of Lindisfarne as any Geordie boy of his age. He knew it was called Holy Island, because hundreds of years ago, monks had lived on it. One of them had been a saint, Saint Cuthbert. And the tide went in and out, making it part of the land twice a day, and an island twice a day. And that was all he knew.

But the very look of the island, with the shadows of clouds drifting across its green hide, spotted like the hide of a cow with brown patches of sand-dunes... it did not look like part of the world, the world of bombs and vicious farmers, and the terrible battle to get enough to eat, and even newspaper to wipe your backside with. He just knew it was an enchanted place, a further shore. He knew he was crossing, not the North Sea but the River Jordan, that the vicar talked about in church. Like Christian, in *The Pilgrim's Progress*, and trumpets would sound for him when he reached the other side.

There was a cottage, as he left the land. A man leaning on his gate, smoking a pipe, called out, "Two hours. You've got a grand day for it."

He didn't know what the man meant; but he waved back cheerfully. The wet sand was firm beneath the Army boots that Artie had given him, and even the joggling pans on his back were merry companions.

Don loved the hugeness of it. Ran ahead, barking for joy. Ran in huge circles, pouncing on bits of seaweed. Charged at the flocks of feeding gulls, sending them exploding into the air like white fireworks.

I'm coming, thought Harry. "I'm coming," he said to the island, all the way across.

The only things that worried him were the two watchtowers. The first he came up to when he was a third of the way across, a gaunt erection of tarred wood piles and rusting iron girders, that thrust itself leaning from the sand. There was a little tarred cabin on top, with a pointed roof, and the legs were thick with barnacles and seaweed. It looked like it had been there a very long time, fighting the waves. There was a thin-runged ladder leading up into it. He took off his gear and climbed the ladder. But the little cabin was completely empty, except people had carved and pencilled names and dates all over the planks inside. And phrases like, "Oh dear, caught again" and, "A bitter cold night". It felt unpleasantly like a prison somehow. It did not feel a happy place. Of course it could not be a prison really; it was obviously to do with the war; it reminded him of the watchtowers the Nazis had round their prison camps. He left it quickly, and did not check up on the other one, half a mile further on.

Then he was on the beach of Lindisfarne itself, with an endless row of sand-dunes on his left. He climbed up one that was higher than the others, and looked ahead. The sand-dunes seemed to go on forever; but there were grey buildings at the end of them, and what looked like ruins.

He went on; he was plodding now; the weight of the pack was starting to cut into his shoulders. Some of the brightness seemed to go out of the morning. Then the sun went behind the clouds. He sat down to rest; and the thought of the pack of sandwiches tempted him. He tried to resist; he'd had a good breakfast; it was just gutsiness. But the thought of the sandwiches went on tormenting him, and finally he thought he'd allow himself just one…

The trouble was, they were ladies' sandwiches, not soldiers' sandwiches. Small and dainty and tasty. He had a second, and a third. Don came up and begged for one trustingly. He knew the rules; what they had, they shared.

Before Harry knew it, nearly all the sandwiches were gone. He closed the packet when there were three left, and shoved them violently back in the pack, with a fury that broke them. He suddenly felt very depressed, and got up and started walking quickly, before he felt any worse. He knew these sudden depressions; they always came when the sun went in.

As he reached the houses, the treacherous sun came out again, and he felt better. But the houses were just a village, like any other village. And the people standing in the cottage doors looked at him in a close, nosy, silent way that he hadn't ever noticed on the mainland. He felt at any moment they were going to ask him what he wanted. He felt if he stopped walking on, looked at all lost, they *would* ask him what he wanted. So he headed on towards the ruins, which at least looked interesting.

He met a man at the gate of the ruins. He would have liked to ask him about Saint Cuthbert. But the man said sharply, "If you're going in there, keep hold of that dog."

He wandered round the ruins, with Don on the leash. Don didn't like that much. He kept on tugging furiously at the leash, wanting to sniff, wanting to be free. Wanting to pee on the old stones as well. He lifted his hind leg twice, and Harry had to drag him away. Because out of the corner of his eyes, he could see the man was still lingering by the gate, watching.

The ruins were quite interesting, especially the single arch of stones that was still in place, that had once helped hold up the long-departed roof. It was so high and pointed and slender, you wondered how it could even hold itself up now. And the stones in the walls were worn by the wind and rain into such strange shapes, like goblins' grinning faces, or squatting fat birds. But you could only stare at stones for so long. Especially when the sun went in again. In the end, they were only *stones*. Then it began to rain.

Next to the ruins was a church that still had the roof on. They ran for it; made it into the porch together. Timidly, Harry tried the great iron ring on the church door. The door swung open silently, on greased hinges. Inside, it was nice, full of bright things, and with a strange sweet smell. And there was a little green baize card-table by the door, with little books stacked on it, called *A Life of Saint Cuthbert*.

Eagerly, he reached for one; opened it. He had always been a keen reader; he missed his books.

"Have you paid for that?"

The voice made Harry jump guiltily. It was the man from the ruins, who must have followed him.

"Not yet," said Harry. "I was just looking."

"Then pay for it, or put it down. We can do wi'out dirty fingerprints all over them."

Harry reached in his pocket, and found a threepenny bit.

"Don't give it to me," said the man. "Can't you read what it says? Put it in that box with the slit in it."

Blushing, Harry looked round for the box. He seemed to have a lot of trouble getting the coin through the slit, with the man glaring at him. Then the man said, "What's the idea, bringing that great dog into a church? Haven't you got any manners? Haven't you been taught the difference between right and wrong?"

"I'll tie him up outside."

"Ye'll not. I don't want him peeing all over the churchyard. And look at all the sand on your boots. It's going all over the floor…"

Harry glared at the man, and the man glared back.

"You're nothing but a little heathen," said the man. "God knows where you were dragged up. You a gypsy or something?" He glanced at the pans dangling from the pack on Harry's back. "Just looking for a chance to steal from the church, were you?"

Harry felt treacherous hot tears starting to gather in the corners of his eyes. He yelled, "Back home, I go to church with my mam twice every Sunday."

"Where's that then?"

"St Peter's, Balkwell."

"Well, get back there, and trail sand all over their floor. See how they like it."

"Suffer the little children to come unto me, and forbid them not, for such is the Kingdom of Heaven," roared Harry. He *had* gone to church twice every Sunday, and a lot of what he'd heard had stuck in his mind.

"Ye what?" shouted the man. "You little toy. How dare you quote scripture at me! I'll belt you on the lug…"

"If anyone should offend these little ones," roared Harry, "it were better that a millstone was hanged around his neck and he was flung into the sea." Once started, he found it very hard to stop, especially when he quarrelled with strange adults.

The man's jaw dropped open. He was speechless. Then he raised his hand for a blow.

Don growled warningly.

"Get out," said the man. "Get out of our church."

Harry got. At the churchyard gate he turned back and shouted, "Call yourself a Christian?"

But it didn't make him feel any better.

And it was worse, when he looked across back to the mainland. The tide had come in. The sand-bridge was gone. Wherever he looked, there were the waves of the shining ocean.

He was cut off.

Suddenly, the whole island felt like a terrible trap. He wanted to sit down and howl. But he knew he had to keep moving. People were still watching him; and some were kids his own age. The school holidays must've started. That's what Ada's mother must've meant last night when she said "a wet week for the start of your holiday". Kids were bad.

He didn't mind the adults so much; all they could do was shout and threaten. But gangs of kids…

He kept walking. He walked round the harbour, and looked at the fishermen, fiddling with their boats. He walked up to a headland with a castle on it. But warning notices kept him from going anywhere near it. And barbed wire. He had never known such an unfriendly place.

And there was a gang of kids following him now. Four of them, and two of them were bigger than he was. They followed him everywhere, pointing at the stuff he was carrying, and taking the mickey and sniggering.

They followed him to the far end of the civilised bit, where the sand-dunes started on the east coast. He had hoped they would leave him alone, if he left their village, but they still followed. When he tried to get back to the village, they stood and blocked his way. And then he realised he had made a bad mistake. Now they could drive him back into the sand-dunes and do what they liked with him, without even their horrible parents interfering.

He walked north up the coast, as fast as he could. They followed at a distance, but closing up slowly. Their voices, on the wind, grew gloating.

They didn't know him; they thought he was running away; what he *was* doing was looking for a weapon, and a place to fight.

Just as they got really near, he found both together.

A ruined boat, from which he snapped a three-yard length of curved rib. It was worn with age, and the end fitted smoothly into his hand. He took off his pack behind the boat, and turned to face them.

They jeered. "Look, he thinks he's Tarzan." But they were suddenly thoughtful; doubtful.

"He's a gypsy. Gypsies don't fight fair!"

"Mebbe he's gotta knife…"

"If he'd gotta knife, he'd have it out, wouldn't he?"

They edged closer, giving sudden jumps towards him, raising their arms, yelling. Judging him, trying to scare him.

He stood his ground, just raising the wooden rib. He'd picked out the leader. The leader was the one he'd try and hit. The leader would come in first, pretending he was the bravest.

They jumped back and forward so much, just avoiding the whistling end of his piece of wood, trying to grab it off him, that when they did really attack, they almost caught him out. He swung up his piece of wood too late.

Except that the leader got in the way of the upswing. It just happened to catch him between the legs. He gave a strangled shriek, and fell writhing on the sand. Harry felt another hand grab for the wood, and tugged it back and lashed out with all his strength, in a panic. It thumped home on somebody else, and there was a proper yelp. Then he was knocked flat, and the wood was held so he couldn't move it, and what felt like a boot hit him agonisingly in the ribs.

And then there was a barking slavering hurricane above him, and the sharp snap of teeth, and another yelp of pain.

And then they were gone. He leapt to his feet, his legs shaking. Saw three of them standing ten yards off. One was clutching his shoulder, like it hurt. Another held a wrist from which blood trickled. And the leader was still trying to crawl in agony, back to his henchmen, doubled up with pain.

They shouted at each other.

"Go and get sticks!"

"Go and get Billie Prudhoe an' his brother! And Alf Green!"

"This bugger's mad. He needs settling for good."

"Tell the poliss. That dog's dangerous. It needs puttin' down."

They picked up their leader, but he kept on doubling up with pain. When he could finally stand unaided, he said, "I'll stay here an' watch him. You fetch the rest of the lads."

Eager to do his bidding, they fled and soon vanished over the sandhills.

Harry knew he was in a jam. The leader was still there.

If Harry made off and tried to hide, the leader would follow him, and summon up his returning gang from the top of the nearest sand-dune… The leader had to be fixed.

He walked towards him. The leader tried to back off. But he was still in pain. Harry caught up with him easily as he tried to scrabble to safety up the side of a sand-dune.

Harry took careful aim, and hit the leader on the ankle with the curving length of wood. With all his force. It was the only way.

There was a nasty crack. The leader yelped, fell down and held his ankle. "Bastard. You've broke it. I'll *kill* you for that."

Harry didn't say a thing. He went back to his gear and picked it up. He called to the dog, and made off up the next slope. The leader made no attempt to follow; he was still nursing his ankle.

He soon dropped from sight.

Harry tried every trick he knew to dodge them. The trouble was, they could follow his footprints in the sand of the sandhills. And especially the dog's; they would be a dead giveaway. So at first he just plunged ahead regardless. Till he came to a little pebbly stream running out of the sandhills to the sea. It gave him an idea.

First he milled around all over the place; but especially where the tall grass grew in clumps, and his footsteps didn't show. When he had made an utter confusion of the whole area and laid a dozen false trails, he got the dog by the collar, and walked him to the sea down the little pebbly stream, where no footprints showed. After that, they walked up to their ankles in the waves, heading north. The gentle breaking waves hid everything. But it was dicey, walking on the open beach. So when another stream came down the sand, he walked the dog up it, and back into the sandhills. After that, all he could do was stick to the bottom of the dunes, the little valleys that ran between them, and hope for the best. He found other lines of footprints; even the prints of another large dog, and that cheered him. There were other people on the dunes; solitary men with binoculars; family groups on holiday with dogs. He kept well clear of them, out of sight. He didn't want them reporting his presence to the gang.

He never saw the gang again. By dusk, with much weary walking up and down through sliding sand, he was back on the beach that led to the sand-bridge. The sand-bridge wasn't far away. It seemed a little narrower than it had been that morning; with little wavelets eating at its edges. But it was still more than two hundred yards across. And he couldn't wait to get off this horrible island.

He and the dog slid like shadows on to the end of the bridge, and vanished into the gathering dark.

Back nearer the village, the wooden warning sign told that the time for a safe crossing was half an hour past.

But he had been careful to go nowhere near the village.

Chapter Fifteen

The trouble was, he was a town child. He believed in roads that stayed as roads, bridges that stayed as bridges. He believed he had a God-given right of way.

He didn't know the sea.

It was not that he was a fool. He kept a sharp eye on the lines of tiny distant breakers on each side of him, that glowed with the white of breaking surf, in the dark. In a way, they were a guide, like the white lines they had painted on the edge of pavements, back home, to guide people when the blackout started.

He began to get the worrying idea that the white lines were getting nearer, but it was hard to judge, in the dark. He hurried as fast as he could, but he was utterly weary; his luggage weighed a ton; the pans banging against his bottom were nagging enemies now. He stopped and looked behind. The cursed island was fading to a low, dim, mottled hump. But in front, the Northumbrian coast seemed no nearer, low, flat, boring. Get on, get on.

Yes, the lines of surf were moving together. The bridge ahead *was* narrower now, seeming little wider than the big wide coast-road at home.

He swung round. Should he make back to the island? He didn't want to. He hated the place. And he was a good way out from it now...

And then, as he watched in horror, a wave more determined than the rest kept on and on, until it had rolled right across the sand-bridge between him and the island. For an awful moment, there was no bridge, just sea. Then the bridge heaved into sight again, like a long whale breaking surface but narrower still.

He looked towards the mainland. The bridge there was still quite wide, unbroken... the way ahead was safer.

He must have run another hundred yards. The very quality of the sand under his feet seemed to be changing, growing wetter, soggier, softer. He was slithering rather than running. His feet couldn't get a grip any more.

And then he saw it. The wave in front that swept right across the sand-bridge...

Frantic, he looked behind again.

There was no sign of the sand-bridge at all. Just the waves rolling across, one after the other.

Run, run, run. The dog ran with him, barking urgently. But he just knew he wasn't going to make it. The world was changing its rules.

He ran into the next wave as it crossed in front; his feet were soaking, icy, in an instant. The sand under them was like freezing porridge. He was waddling slowly like a duck.

And the mainland looked as far away as ever.

It came to him that he was going to drown. There was no way that he couldn't drown. He couldn't run a mile; he couldn't run fifty yards.

And the next crossing wave was half-way to his knees, and strong. He felt the tug of it.

And now the whole sand-bridge was gone for good. Even between waves it wasn't showing. Where had all the water come from so quickly? He couldn't even work out which way to go any more. He was standing up to his ankles in the whole wide trackless sea. He felt dizzy, as the endless waves moved past him, with their burden of sand. The ground seemed to be moving under him, sucking his feet away. He nearly fell, and there was nothing to hang on to in the whole moving world.

He gave one last despairing gaze around.

And then he saw it. Leaning crookedly out of the sea, dimly dark against the moving waves.

The watchtower. The second watchtower. He remembered, oddly, the writings scratched inside the walls of the first watchtower. "Caught again", "A bitter cold night".

The tower was a refuge for people trapped by the tide. Before it became really clear in his mind, he was floundering towards it.

The waves were up to his knees now, really pushing him away towards the left. There were deeper bits, where the water sloshed up, freezing him between the legs, freezing him up so he had no feeling. He had to keep looking for the watchtower, because the waves were pushing him off course. And all the time the dog was alongside, barking joyously, thinking it was another game. He fell full-length, hauled himself back upright with a choking scream, fell again, and the waves rolled over him. Scrambling, crawling, underwater, then a lungful of air that ended in water again. But the tower was looming up...

A huge wave, that drove the dog sideways into him, so they went down in a flailing tangle. Up, breathing, screaming, gargling, drowning...

And then something hard and solid banged against his head. He grabbed, and he had it. Worked sideways towards the bottom of the ladder, hanging on like a limpet as the waves hit him.

Foot of the ladder, climb, climb. His soaking clothes dragged him back; his gear was like a heavy hand on his shoulders.

He pushed open the door, and collapsed inside. He waited for the dog to arrive, and land on top of him. No dog. Still no dog.

He swung round and looked down. In the darkness, he could see the dog's head, and only the dog's head, at the bottom of the ladder. It wasn't standing any more; it was swimming now. As he looked, a wave swept the head away to one side. He screamed.

"Don!"

Then he saw the dog, in between waves, trying to swim back. Why hadn't it climbed the ladder after him?

And then he realised; the ladder was too steep; the rungs were rusted away too thin. No way could a big dog like Don climb it, especially from swimming in the sea.

Don was going to drown. He was a good swimmer, but he was too far from land. And the waves were big… and the dog wouldn't leave him to save itself. It was being killed by its own faithfulness.

Something inside him snapped. The dog was the other half of him. The dog was the last person he had left.

Without the dog the world would be… empty.

You shan't have him! You shan't have him as well! Or you might as well have me too! Screaming swear-words at he knew not what, he threw off the burden on his back and went pell-mell down the ladder, into the sea. It was deep now. It came up to his shoulders; its cold, entering the coldness of his own body, flooded him, took all his breath away. But when he opened his eyes, he saw the head of the dog, swimming up to him again, just a dark blob with two depressed ears, against the low glow of the breaking surf.

He grabbed its collar, and the ladder doubly hard, as he felt the muscular swell of the next wave coming in to hit them. He thought his arms had been pulled off his body, but when the wave passed, the dog was still close to him, its hair floating queerly in the water, tickling his hand.

"Up, boy." He heaved the dog at the ladder. It scrabbled at the thin iron rung with its front feet, not able to get a grip.

He knew there was only one thing to do, and he did it without thinking. He took a breath, ducked underwater, got his shoulder under the dog's broad haunch and heaved.

By the time the next wave hit him, he was standing upright on the sand with both hands on the ladder, and the dog, an incredible weight, was standing on his shoulders, clear of the water.

It scrabbled above him. But it couldn't get any higher. As the next wave came, he put one foot on the ladder, and tried a step up.

The lifting power of the wave did it. His leg muscles screamed with pain, but he made the step up.

Waiting for the next big wave, timing it just right, he made another step up. And a third.

But with every step up, the lifting power of the waves decreased. He stuck on the third step. He couldn't make the fourth. His hands were going numb with cold; he couldn't feel his legs.

He felt the huge wave coming. It must be two steps this time or nothing. That was all he was ever going to be able to manage.

It was a very huge wave. Spluttering like a maniac, he managed one, two, then, incredibly, three. It was impossible, but he did it. The next second, he felt a tremendous convulsive kick from the dog's hind legs. Then no weight at all... And he knew he'd failed, and could never do it again. Don, Don! He hung on, blinded by sea-water, not wanting to do anything ever again. Let go. Let the sea take you. No more trying, no more pain.

Then a burst of barking hit his ears, as the sea-water drained from them. he looked up, and the dog's head was sticking out of the open door...

It was quite easy after that. He only had to rest between every step he took.

It was not so bad. The two blankets in the middle of his bedroll were only damp. He stripped and rubbed himself down with them, then wrapped them round himself. He would have liked to rub the dog down too, but there was nothing else left dry to do it with. There were nails knocked in the walls of the hut, and he wrung out his clothes and hung them to dry. Some hope!

For the sea was still rising, climbing the rungs of the ladder, one by one, inexorably. He wondered, quite calmly, if the tide ever rose so high, the waves ever grew so wild, that the refuge on top was entirely submerged. If so, there was nothing he could do about it.

And the sea sent its messengers before it. The very air he breathed was full of salty spray, so that he breathed a mixture of air and water, half boy, half fish. And the bigness of the sea overwhelmed him; the bigness of the sound of it. The land seemed so far away, it was nowhere. Nothing but sea. The sound of the waves did not soothe him. The sea had tried to kill him. Might still kill him. Meanwhile, he watched it.

In the end, with bitter satisfaction, he watched it lose its force, like a beaten army, and start to retreat, rung by rung.

Only then did he curl up in the two blankets and fall asleep.

Sunlight wakened him, falling in through the half-open door on to his face. He tried getting up, and could hardly move, he was so cut and bruised and stiff. He peered out at his enemy.

The enemy was nowhere to be seen. Nothing but flat sand, steaming gently in the sun. Seaweed. Feeding gulls. A mottled duck leading her mottled chicks to drink at a stream of fresh water that flowed across the sands.

He realised how thirsty he was. But he'd have to get dressed first; those thin rusty ladder rungs would cut his bare feet to ribbons.

As they must have cut Don's paw last night. The dog was lying looking at him, still half-soaked, its fur in great wet lumps. It was licking its paw, and red blood showed.

Jesus, he'd got Don up last night. How on earth was he going to get him down? The sand looked dizzying miles away...

Shivering, he dragged on his damp clothes.

It was only then that he realised the precious attaché case had gone.

He didn't even remember dropping it, in the fight against drowning. All the insurance policies, and all the ration books, and the little bottle of brandy. The last of Mam and Dad and

Dulcie. And Dad's watch, that he only wore for best...

Still, he was thirsty, so he climbed down and had a drink. It was such a calm, warm, lovely morning... but for once the lovely morning didn't work. He just kept thinking about the attaché case and feeling totally guilty and miserable.

Don barked at him, hopelessly, absurdly, from the door of the watchtower. How *was* he going to get him down?

And yet that solved itself so easily. A man with a horse and cart, coming across the sands.

"Hey, kid, what's that dog doing up there?"

"He's my dog. We got caught by the tide last night."

"Want me to fetch him down for you?"

"Please."

He was a huge man. The biggest man Harry had ever seen. He just climbed up the ladder, spoke to the dog, heaved him over his shoulder, and climbed down with him. On his shoulder, Don didn't look much bigger than a fox-terrier.

"You wanta get that dog's paw seen to. It's a bad cut."

Then he was off across the sands again.

A miracle. But it didn't make Harry feel any better. He began to worry about getting Don to a vet. Felt for the banknotes he always carried in the right-hand pocket of his raincoat...

A shapeless sodden wad of green paper, that he had to

squeeze the water out of. He tried to peel off a note, and it began to tear.

He didn't even feel like crying. He was beyond crying. He didn't feel he had any tears left in him. He didn't feel he had any blood left in him.

But they had to get ashore. The man had told him he only had an hour.

Half-way to the shore, he saw something brown and square in the middle of a rock-pool. It couldn't possibly be… But it was. The attaché case. It was a morning for miracles. But strangely, that didn't make him feel any better either. The miracles were coming too late. Especially as, when he picked up the attaché case, it was far too heavy and deluged water out of the corners.

Inside, everything was sodden, ruined. But he wearily picked it up and plodded on.

They reached the land. They went as far as the main road. But Don was limping worse and worse, so they went and sat down on the grass by the roadside. He got Don to show him his paw. The dog was very reluctant. The gash was still bleeding, and full of sand, muck and little stones. Don wouldn't let him take the stones out; it must hurt too much.

So they just went on sitting and sitting. While the tide came in, and began to go out again.

Harry just felt that his own personal tide had gone out forever. It was never coming back. It was all no good. He had fought and schemed and walked and gathered sea-coal all these weeks, and now they were worse off than ever. It was no good trying any more. No matter how hard you fought everything just went wrong in the end. The chip shop at Tynemouth, the stay with Joseph, Artie, his own little pillbox, Lindisfarne, the further shore. All… useless. Look at Ada's mother, all that adventure and cheerfulness and flying and climbing mountains, and now she was just a fat old lady falling downstairs and waiting to die.

Everybody died in the end. He wished they'd drowned last night. By now, all his troubles would be over…

Even the airman's marvellous watch had stopped, the water-glass dewed with droplets.

With that thought in mind, he fell asleep.

He never noticed the man.

The man had been noticing him for some time. He was in a tiny Austin Seven. He had passed once, and seen Harry sitting there. When he passed again, an hour later, Harry was still sitting in the same place.

The man took much more interest this time.

The third time the man drove past, Harry was lying on the grass verge asleep. And Don was sitting holding up his bloody paw helplessly, and watching the passing traffic.

The man drove past Harry.

Then stopped his car with a tiny squeal of brakes. He seemed to sit for a long time, hands on the wheel, as if he was having an inner argument with himself. Then he banged his hands on the steering wheel, as if he'd made up his mind to do something. Then he backed the car slowly to where Harry was lying. And got out.

Chapter Sixteen

Harry came awake in a blur. At first he thought he was in bed at home, and it was Mam shaking his shoulder. He opened his eyes, and there was this man's face, a total stranger's face, saying something he couldn't understand. Over and over again.

He looked round desperately. He was in the open air, in a totally strange place he couldn't even remember coming to. Panic surged inside him. The man said the same thing again. And again. What was he *saying*?

With a last despairing effort, Harry focused his concentration.

"Your dog's hurt," said the man. "You must get him to a vet."

He looked at the man's face. The man flinched and looked away. At the sky. At the sea. Anywhere but at Harry. What a strange man…

The man looked at him again; a fleeting, almost guilty glance. "Can I look at the dog's paw?" he said, looking at Don.

"Yes," said Harry. He couldn't understand this man at all. Maybe Don would understand him. He trusted Don's judgement. If Don let the man touch him, the man must be all right.

Don let the man touch him. Let him stroke his ears. The man talked to Don in a gentle voice, calling him "boy". Then he raised the hurt paw gently. Again, Don let him. The man looked at the paw, then let go of it. Don licked the man's face, with his long pinky-purple tongue. The man came back, his face serious.

"We *must* get him to a vet. That gash won't heal itself. He could lose his foot. He could *die*."

"OK!" said Harry. He didn't understand anything except about Don's paw.

The man helped Harry to his feet. His touch was soft, like a woman's; his hands were strong enough, but they trembled. Harry knew the man was terribly excited about something.

The man put Harry into the seat next to the driver's

seat. Then he pulled forward the driver's seat, and piled all Harry's gear on to the back seat, The stuff dripped all over the cracked leather of the back seat, but Harry was beyond caring. Then the man coaxed Don into the back seat, next to Harry's stuff, got in himself, and they were off. Not very fast. The car was little and old, and the engine sounded weak, as if it might give out at any moment. The windscreen was all yellowed round the edges, and there was some kind of silver dial on the front of the bonnet. The man drove silently, keeping his eyes on the road. His hands were very white and tight on the wheel. All he said was, "That cut paw's bad, very bad. We must get it seen to, straightaway." He said it four times without looking at Harry at all. As if to himself.

The vet's was more reassuring. A big house with a big brass plate saying "John Harper MRCVS", very highly polished, but with dried Brasso in the lettering. Inside, there was highly polished brown lino, and it smelt like a hospital.

The vet came bristling in, in his white coat, which had pale pink washed-out stains down the front.

"Now, now, what have we here?" He lifted Don on to the table, played with his ears a bit, then lifted the foot and said, "That's a nasty one. How'd he get that?"

"On an iron ladder," said Harry in a very small voice. Then added, "Is he going to be all right?"

"Be a big job," said the vet. "I'll have to chloroform him before I can see to it. And I'll have to keep him in for a few days. He'll have to be kept still."

Harry despaired. "How much will that cost?"

"You can leave that to me," said the man with the car. He gabbled it, like he was saying something shameful.

"Right, Mr Murgatroyd," said the vet. There was something odd in his voice, as he said it. It wasn't *dislike*. It was more pity. As if Mr Murgatroyd had a wooden leg, or was deformed or something. "Right then. We'd better get on with it straightaway. Sooner it's done, the better." And he picked up Don, and carried him away through an open door, without even giving Harry a chance to say goodbye. "Give me a call this evening, Mr Murgatroyd, and I'll let you know how he's got on."

And suddenly, Harry and Mr Murgatroyd were outside and back at the car. Without Don, Harry was suddenly terribly embarrassed. He could think of nothing to say, but went on staring at the little silver dial on the bonnet of the car. Mr Murgatroyd didn't seem to know what to say either. Then Harry reached in his raincoat pocket, and felt the wet wodge of notes.

"I've got money," he said. "Only it's all stuck together."

"How'd you mean?" asked Mr Murgatroyd with a sudden burst of enthusiasm, as if he was glad he'd found something to say.

Harry showed him. "If I wait till they're dry, I might be able to…"

"No, no," said Mr Murgatroyd. "The way to separate them is to make them *wetter*. Come on, I'll show you." And he bundled Harry back into the car, as if there was nothing in his life at all half so important as separating some banknotes.

It was quite a long drive, full of twists and turns. Long enough to convince Harry he could never find his way back to Don on his own. Then they were arriving at a big grey stone farmhouse, with windows each side of a blue door. But the man drove up the cobbles at the side, to the back door.

There was a large black and white cat sitting on the back doorstep. She came forward to greet Mr Murgatroyd with a loud miaow, her bushy black tail vertical. Mr Murgatroyd bent to stroke her, and started a long conversation.

"Dinnertime, is it, Mrs Murgatroyd? Not really, you know. You're half an hour early, you scheming puss. You won't go to Heaven, telling such lies. You'll go down *there*, where the great Dog will gobble you up. Why don't you go and catch your own dinner for once? Plenty of fat mice round the barns. Only you'd rather sit in the sun and be a kept woman…"

And so on, and so forth, as if he was never going to stop.

And the cat talked back to him, non-stop too, in a series of prooks and miaows, striding backwards and forwards, while he gently pulled her tail, until Harry could have died with embarrassment.

Then Mr Murgatroyd clapped his hand to his forehead, said, "Banknotes", and dashed indoors. He filled an enamel basin in the sink from the cold tap, and took the solid wodge of notes and dropped them in. Harry watched anxiously, while they just *floated*, waiting for them to dissolve into pure sludge at any moment. Fourteen pounds ten shillings; four weeks' wages for a grown man. He wondered if Mr Murgatroyd was some kind of lunatic. The silence between them deepened and deepened.

"Fancy a mug of tea?" asked Mr Murgatroyd suddenly.

"Yes, please." Well, at least that got rid of him and his terrible silence. It was all right while he was clinking and bustling round the kitchen.

"Right," said Mr Murgatroyd. Harry turned, and saw a tray set not only with a mug of tea, but a neat embroidered little traycloth, and a plate with three huge slices of fruitcake.

"Help yourself to sugar."

Harry stirred in three spoonfuls; the sight of all that cake made his stomach erupt as if it was full of fizzing soda-pop.

"Eat up all the cake if you want. It's Christmas cake really. It needs finishing up." Mr Murgatroyd settled into a chair, and watched Harry eat. Why was he watching so closely? As if he was counting every crumb. He'd said it could all be eaten up… he was a *jumpy* person, sitting on the edge of his chair. Harry suddenly grew ashamed because his hands weren't all that clean.

"Sorry, my hands are dirty…"

"Don't worry about that," said Mr Murgatroyd. "Don't worry about that at all. Not important. Not important." Then he got up and dashed from the room, as if he'd been shot. Through the window, Harry saw him talking to the cat again. Then, the next time he looked, Mr Murgatroyd had got hold of a spade and was frantically digging up a patch of garden.

Harry finished all the cake; even gathered the crumbs together with his finger-end and ate them. Then he drained the tea to the last drop. And still felt ravenously hungry. But it was all gone. So he drifted over to the window above the sink. Through the window, he could see Mr Murgatroyd had finished digging the patch of earth, and was now frantically nailing up a bit of fence.

Then he looked down.

A miracle. Three pound notes had floated free; they were nearly transparent with wet, but clear of the wodge. As he looked, another one began to curl free of the wodge… Mr Murgatroyd wasn't as mad as he seemed. Harry tried to lift one of the floating notes out of the water. It tore nearly all the way across.

"No, no," said Mr Murgatroyd, appearing suddenly at his elbow. "A fish-slice and blotting paper."

He had come in so silently, Harry jumped a foot in the air. His heart still seemed to be pounding as he watched Mr M. fish out the last note safely.

"Put them by the fire. By the fire. Face upwards. Then even if they stick to the blotting paper, the bank manager can still read the signature, and will give you a new one."

Harry had an awful vision of himself walking into a bank...

"Don't worry," said Mr M. kindly. "I'll take them to the bank for you in the morning."

"Thanks." He gave Mr M. a smile.

"Don't thank me. No need for thanks." Mr M.'s eyes were everywhere but Harry's face. "Anything else you want dried out – the stuff in the car – get it for you." He fled again, and returned panting with all the stuff. "Get you a clothes-horse – then you can see to things yourself. I'll make up the fire – good fire, good fire." Then he was off outdoors again.

Harry hung what he could over the old wooden clothes-horse. He laid the contents of the attaché case, and the case itself, out on the clippie rug before the fire, where they steamed gently. Then there was nothing to do. He watched Mr M. out of the window. Leading a pair of goats past the gate; feeding a small flock of geese, and talking, talking to them. Mr M. seemed to talk to everything that moved. Harry wondered if he was barmy, like old Joseph. He didn't *look* barmy. Tall and thin, with a grey nibbled moustache and short-cut hair. His clothes were worn, but he looked very clean and neat. And he did everything very efficiently round the farm, and what he did seemed to make sense.

Then there were all the books. Lots of bookshelves. More books piled neatly in the corners of the room. Big serious books, mainly history, but some poetry too. And a pile of war-magazines, in strict order of date, so that Harry hardly dared touch them. But the last one was badly out of date – six months old, and the top was thick with dust.

He suddenly felt very tired again. He curled up in the big armchair by the fire, with the last magazine. He remembered it from home; he and Dad had bought the same magazine.

But the last copy was a miserable one. January 1942, and the sinking of the *Repulse* and *Prince of Wales* by those Japanese bombers... had Mr M. stopped buying the magazine then, because it was such a miserable number, full of bad news? The news had got better since then.

Since the Battle of Midway, the Japs were on the run...

He slept.

"Wakey, wakey," said Mr M. "Teatime. It's just bacon and eggs, but there's plenty of it."

There was too. Two eggs and huge rashers of thick-cut bacon, swimming in their own golden grease. And a pile of thick-cut white bread. And butter with dewdrops coming out of it.

"That's a whole week's ration," gasped Harry. "Two weeks' rations."

"Not round here. I know the farmers. Plenty if you know the farmers – I teach their sons. I don't go short."

With a nervous flick of the eyes, Mr M. vanished behind a copy of *Picture Post*. A six-month-old copy of *Picture Post*. He seemed able to eat and read at the same time, though from the tilt of his grey head, visible above the magazine, he wasn't getting on very well with the article he was reading.

"Rang the vet," he said, with his mouth full. "Your dog's OK. Just coming round from the chloroform nicely. Vet says you can go and see him tomorrow – I'll run you down there."

"Oh, *thanks*," said Harry. "Thanks for being so kind."

A fit of coughing broke out behind *Picture Post*. It went on and on. It appeared a large morsel of food had gone down the wrong way. Mr M. dropped the magazine on to his greasy plate, and sat coughing helplessly, tears streaming down his face. Harry, alarmed he was going to choke to death, ran round and banged him firmly on the back.

"Thanks," said Mr M. when the coughing had subsided at last.

Abruptly, the painful silence fell again. Harry had never known a silence like it. It was scarcely endurable. It hung in the room like a great dark threatening shadow. Making the tick of the clock far too loud. Every crack of the fire made you jump.

"Fancy a walk?" said Mr M. abruptly. "I always have a walk before bed."

The clock on the wall said seven o'clock...

Harry thought suddenly that Mr M. was having a fight with time itself. The same as he was having this terrible fight with silence. A silence that was choking him. Only... you couldn't fight with *time*. You couldn't fight with *silence*.

It was as if... Harry struggled... as if there was another person in the house. An invisible person who was frightening Mr M. out of his wits, using the weapons of time and silence.

Only that was *mad*. A mad thought. Was Mr M. mad? Or was he going mad himself? Not a nice thought either way...

"Yes, I'll come for a walk," said Harry.

Mr M. set off at a great pace, so that Harry, still tired, had a great job in keeping up. Mr M. had an old battered pair of binoculars hung round his neck. He walked so fast they must have banged against his chest painfully.

But it was a glorious evening, and they walked to the sea. Lindisfarne lay low and golden. The sea was in, and the two refuge-towers stuck out of it. They stopped to admire the view, and Harry managed to get his breath back. Then he said, "We nearly drowned, coming back from there. That's why everything got so wet."

"I thought it might be something like that," said Mr M. He didn't seem all that interested. "Look, there's a fulmar. He comes every evening, about this time, and flies round and round this bit of cliff. Exactly the same pattern every time. I think he's just showing off."

It was almost a joke. And he did seem a little calmer. And the longer they walked, the calmer he got. He seemed to know a lot about birds and plants and explained about them, in a way that was eager, and not at all show-off. It was a bit like going for a walk with Artie, only Mr M. knew longer Latin names for things. There were still silences, but they didn't drill into your brain, like they did in the house.

Only one odd thing happened, as they walked back through the village, having come off the cliffs. There was an old man, standing smoking at his cottage door.

"Evening, Mr Murgatroyd!" His tone was kind, but there was that same kind of weary pity in it. Again, as if Mr M. had a wooden leg, or was deformed or something…

"Evening, Sam. How's your lad?" There was a sudden tightness, as of pain, in Mr M.'s voice.

"Doing fine," said the old man. "Making fourteen pound a week, in that Vickers factory at Newcastle. Churning out tanks like cans of beans they are, every hour God sends. He hardly has time to write. He's still keen to do his bit for his country. But he's in that controlled occupation."

For a moment, the old man sounded ashamed. Then he said, "Nice to see you with a young 'un, Mr Murgatroyd. Like old times, eh?"

The sudden, silent cold was back. Harry, glancing at Mr M., thought he looked ten years older, all of a sudden.

Then Mr M. just said, "Goodnight, Sam," and walked on.

"Everything's dry now," said Harry. Then he screwed up his courage and said, "Can I sleep in your barn tonight?" He didn't know what else to say. It was getting dark outside, and he had to make *some* arrangements.

"You'll do no such thing," said Mr M. "There's a bed upstairs for you, if you want it. First room on the left. And if you want a bath, there's plenty of hot water. Bathroom second on the right. Now I must go and fasten up the geese."

And he was gone again, before Harry could say thank you.

So all Harry could do was go upstairs, taking his dried things with him.

The bed was neatly turned down, and there were striped pyjamas laid out ready for him. Again they were a bit big for him; but they were certainly far too small for Mr M.

And a towel, and a half-used bar of soap, and a half-used tube of toothpaste.

It was strange, having a hot bath again, and even stranger getting into somebody else's worn pyjamas, twice in three nights.

But the bed was soft, and he soon fell asleep.

Chapter Seventeen

Harry was awakened by the rattling of a cup and saucer outside his bedroom door. It was a really terrible rattling, as if Mr M. was shaking himself to pieces.

Then there was a long, long pause, and that same terrible silence. When Harry felt he couldn't really take any more, and almost called out, the door opened.

Mr M. stood there, fully clad. He had the cup and saucer in one hand, and a bundle of clothes under his other arm. That much Harry saw through the lashes of his near-closed eyes, for he felt it was wiser to pretend to be still asleep.

Mr M. stood looking at Harry a very long time. At first, a slow smile crept across his face. Then, slowly, it faded; Mr M.'s face grew sadder and sadder, until Harry almost cried out again, just to stop it getting worse.

At that point, Mr M. crossed the room on tiptoe, put the rattling cup on the bedside table and draped the clothes over a chair. There were corduroy trousers, a check shirt, vest and underpants and socks. And last, a blue jumper. Mr M. arranged the clothes with little tugs, and then rearranged them again. Satisfied, he tiptoed to the door, and looked at Harry's face again. With a stare so intense that Harry felt he was being eaten, *alive*. Then he made a dash for Harry's old clothes, where he had dropped them carelessly on the floor. He snatched them up, avidly, and vanished from the room. Calling as he went, suddenly, "Wakey wakey. Rise and shine."

Feeling rather shaky himself, Harry swung his legs down to the floor, and drank the cup of tea. It had three sugars in. When he whipped out to the loo, there was the smell of frying bacon, coming upstairs. So he thought he'd better get washed and dressed quickly.

Mr M. seemed to have finished his breakfast. He was stuck behind the morning's *Times*. He said, shortly, "Your breakfast's in the oven."

It was bacon and eggs again, but Harry wasn't grumbling. After what he'd been through, he could eat bacon and eggs like that forever. He even mopped up the greasy plate with bread.

"There's toast there," said Mr M. in a tight voice. Harry munched his way through a lot of toast and marmalade. Then he felt guilty again, because of the rationing.

"Is it all right if I finish it up?"

Mr M.'s face appeared fleetingly. He smiled, as if he was really pleased. "I like a boy who eats a good breakfast," he said. "You need feeding up." Then his face vanished again.

Harry stared at the large headlines of the paper. There had been a victory in the Western Desert, at a place called Alam Halfa. Field Marshal Montgomery seemed to have destroyed a lot of Rommel's tanks.

"Monty's given Rommel what-for then!" said Harry.

Mr M.'s hands tightened on the paper. "I never discuss the war," he said, in a very small voice. Then he seemed to relent and lowered the paper and said, "We'd better go down and see how your dog's getting on."

The car rattled and creaked along. And Mr M. rattled on non-stop about what a marvellous vet Mr Harper was. How animals loved him, how cats twined round him, purring, even when he was giving them injections. So it was a bit of an anti-climax to find, when they arrived, that Mr Harper was out on his rounds. They were shown into the back area by a bad-tempered woman in an overall, who seemed to regard them as a nuisance. Don was in a pen, on a bed of old blankets. He seemed sleepy, and didn't get up, though his tail beat against the floor. They both went in and stroked him. Harry thought again how good Mr M. was with animals, and how bad he was with people.

"He's all right," said Mr M., still stroking Don. "He's just sleepy after the anaesthetic." Don's paw was tightly and neatly bandaged, but Harry was a bit worried that there was a little blood seeping through the bandage.

"'Saright," said Mr M. "Harper knows what he's doing."

Then they were back in the car, with the silence growing between them, and the whole empty sunny day stretching ahead with nothing to do.

Harry thought hard. He was getting increasingly nervous about what Mr M. wanted him for. All adults wanted *something*. Joseph had wanted help with beachcombing; the old lady had wanted to... well, Artie had wanted things fetched from the NAAFI.

"Can I help?" he said diffidently, not looking at Mr M., just staring through the windscreen at the little silver dial on the bonnet.

"Help?" said Mr M. He sounded most surprised. "Help with what?"

"I could do the washing-up," said Harry. "I helped my mam with the washing-up. I didn't break anything..."

"Bless the boy," said Mr M. to nobody in particular.

"Yes, you can do the washing-up if you like…"

"And can I help you with the farm… with the animals?"

"It's not a farm," said Mr M. "I've only got four acres. Goats, hens, geese. But you can help if you like." He seemed happier. He rattled on in great detail about goats, hens, and geese all the way home. It was as if Harry had opened a floodgate.

Mr M. was right. It wasn't a farm; it was more like a zoo. There were three she-goats, and Harry had a go at milking Emily, the quiet one. There was also a very nasty billy-goat who spent all his time getting behind your back, so he could butt you.

"He hasn't got a very nice nature," said Mr M. "But he was born here, and I couldn't bear to send him to market. He's got a right to live, like anything else. I'm against Death." He said it as if Death was a person, to be outwitted. And he was so against Death that he spent ten minutes in the hen-cree with a jam jar, trying to catch a wasp so he could put it safely out of the door.

"I just swat wasps," said Harry. "But I'd never swat a bee." He remembered spending ten minutes rescuing a bee in their kitchen at home, with a jam jar, in just the same way.

"Never kill anything you can't create," said Mr M. "Who gave you the power of life and death?"

"What about germs?" asked Harry. Mr M. was silent for a long time after that, and Harry was sorry he'd been so smart-aleck. But it was a happy day on the whole, because they worked side by side, never looking each other in the face. Mr M. never looked people in the face. But he talked non-stop to make up. Harry could see that he really was a teacher. And he had given all the animals names. Not just the four cats, but every goose; even every hen. He knew everything about them.

"That hen hurt her leg one night, when I left her out of the cree by mistake. She can stand on two legs, but she only hops on one."

"That black cat is the black and white one's kitten. He never left home. She still washes him every night, though he's twice her size. But she gets fed up with him sometimes and bites him on the neck when he's lying asleep."

It was as if it was a kingdom of animals, and Mr M. was the king.

On the third morning, Harry, coming downstairs, heard a woman's voice in the kitchen. His hand was on the kitchen door-handle, when he heard the woman's voice say, shrilly, "You can't *do* that, Mr Murgatroyd! It's not right! It's downright *wicked*!"

Mr M.'s voice was too low to make out what he said in reply.

"He must have a mother and a father somewhere! Who must be worried sick about him!" said the woman.

Harry stayed frozen, silent. They were talking about *him*.

Mr M.'s voice murmured.

The woman's voice rose higher. "You know what happened the last time. The police warned you. You coulda lost your job. You coulda gone to *prison*."

Murmur, murmur.

"I'll not stay in a house with such wickedness. I'm giving my notice. I'll not be a party to it."

There were the sounds of movement. Just in time, Harry fled back upstairs. From the top of the stairs, he watched the woman storm out, buttoning up her coat. Timidly, he went downstairs again.

Mr M. sat with his head in his hands, unmoving. Harry just stood, watching. He seemed to watch forever. He had never seen anyone sit like that.

In the end, he said timidly, "Are you all right?"

Mr M. looked up, as if he did not know where he was. He was holding a photograph in a frame. Silently, he held it out to Harry.

It was a photograph of a boy, laughing. A boy a bit older than Harry.

But he was wearing a checked shirt, a blue pullover, corduroy trousers.

The clothes Harry was wearing now.

Harry looked up.

Mr M. had his head in his hands again.

"Who was he?" asked Harry. But he knew; the boy looked so much like Mr Murgatroyd.

"He was fourth-top in his year at Dartmouth. He nearly won the sword of honour. He was only eighteen. Eighteen, five months and four days. He was a midshipman. George Frederick Murgatroyd. His friends called him Freddy. He was on the *Repulse*. You know what happened to the *Repulse*?"

"I remember," said Harry.

"They never even reached their target. Sheer waste. Sheer bloody waste."

Then, tight-lipped, he took the photo off Harry, and put it back in the cupboard and locked the door. "Must go and see to the hens…"

"What did you nearly get put in prison for?" Harry didn't think it was the right time to ask. But he had to know.

Mr Murgatroyd sat down again. "There was a boy. I was fond of him. He came here often. He was miserable at home. His father hit him a lot. One night, he came to me;

he was all bleeding. He said he wouldn't go home any more. I said he could... stay here. His father came for him... I threw the drunken sot out of my house..."

"Yes," said Harry feelingly, "yes."

"The parents came back with a policeman... they accused me of enticing the boy... trying to steal their son. I had to let them have him. I could've lost my job. I could've gone to prison. It's a crime, you see, enticement."

"Yes," said Harry.

"Why did they *want* him," said Mr M., "if they hated him so much? Don't they realise how *precious* sons are?" He said it softly, but it was like a scream.

Harry took a deep breath, and said, "My parents are dead. They were killed in the bombing. I haven't got nobody."

"It's no good," said Mr M. "That woman... Mrs Cleve... my cleaning lady... she'll gossip. I'll be the talk of the village. Somebody will tell the police... villages are like that."

"Couldn't you talk to her...?"

"She won't listen to me."

Harry got up. "Perhaps she'll listen to *me*. Where does she live?"

Mr M. told him, in a low voice, then put his head back in his hands. He seemed to be beyond caring.

* * *

Harry knocked on Mrs Cleve's front door and waited. He knocked again, but there was still no answer. But he wasn't in any mood to go away. So he barged round the back, and found Mrs Cleve hanging out washing, her mouth full of clothes pegs.

They stared at each other. Harry thought Mrs Cleve didn't have an unkind face; just a worried one. And, like Mam, worry would make her hasty. She would do things in a rush and be sorry after. Mrs Cleve needed slowing down.

"Please," said Harry. "Can I have a drink of water? I feel faint."

Mrs Cleve bustled him into the kitchen, and sat him in a chair, and made him put his head between his knees. Harry didn't mind. She wouldn't just chuck him out of her kitchen like she might have chucked him out of her garden. After a little while, he said he'd stopped feeling faint. Pleased with herself, Mrs Cleve said, "I'll give you something better than water," and went and brought a glass of home-made lemon barley. Harry sipped it slowly, playing for time; waiting for Mrs Cleve to finally get out of her flap and start to feel nosy. His dad had always said that all women were nosy.

Finally he said, "This is lovely. Just like me mam used to make."

"*Used* to?" Mrs Cleve was on to that like a flash.

"Me mam's dead." Harry watched the look on Mrs Cleve's face change. He was no longer in any danger of being thought an impudent young pup, or a damned young nuisance. He was now, in Mrs Cleve's mind, "that poor wee bairn".

"Your mam can't have been any great age?" said Mrs Cleve cautiously.

"She was killed in the bombing. On Tyneside. Two months ago." Careful, don't rush her.

"So you and your dad'll be managing on your own?"

"Me dad was killed too. By the same bomb." And while Mrs Cleve's face crumpled up with horror, he added, "And me little sister." Was it terrible, to use their memories like this? But you had to survive. Mam and Dad would've wanted him to *survive*.

"How did you escape?" asked Mrs Cleve, a tinge of suspicion still in her voice.

"We was down the shelter. Me an' me dog. We always went down first, to get things ready."

"Haven't you got *nobody*?"

"Just the dog." He wasn't going to mention Cousin Elsie. Cousin Elsie would be a very bad mistake. "Mr Murgatroyd was very kind when the dog hurt his foot. He took him to the vet's. He's still there, till his foot gets better."

"How've you *managed*?" Mrs Clever was really hooked now, her eyes wide as saucers, her mouth slightly parted.

"Sleeping rough. Till Mr Murgatroyd found me. He's very kind."

"He's too kind for his own good," said Mrs Cleve, her voice softening. "He's never been the same since that lad of his was killed off in Malaya."

"What happened to *him*?" asked Harry innocently.

And Mrs Cleve was off... Mr Murgatroyd's long sufferings, the death of his wife five years ago; bringing up the boy on his own; the boy's death; the other boy, the trouble with the police... And all the time Mrs Cleve's voice got softer, and several times she paused, to wipe her eyes on her flowery pinafore. Harry did nothing but sigh and look incredulous. For hours and hours. In the end, she stopped.

Now was the crucial time. The idea must come from Mrs Cleve...

"I must be going," said Harry. "Thank you very much for the nice lemonade." He got up.

"Going? Going where?" said Mrs Cleve.

"Back on the road. I mustn't get Mr Murgatroyd into any more trouble."

"But how will you *manage*?"

"I'll manage. I managed before."

"But you're only a bairn… there should be people looking after you."

"They'd put me in a home," said Harry. "And they'd put my dog to sleep. And the dog's the only thing I've got left. Goodbye. Thank you for the lemonade…"

Mrs Cleve looked bewildered. She passed a hand across her face. "Eeh, it doesn't bear thinking about. Little bits o' bairns… here, sit down while I put my thinking cap on. I'll make you a cup of tea. And there's some seedy cake left. Eeh, have some tea while I gather me wits…"

Harry sat and let himself be fed, while Mrs Cleve bustled about saying things like, "I don't know what the world's coming to!" and "Hitler and his bloody Germans!" Finally she announced, "We'll have to go and talk to Mr Murgatroyd. Hang on a minute while I put on my coat and hat."

Harry waited, and was content to wait. Mrs Cleve was in the conspiracy now, up to her neck.

"Well," said Mr M. when Mrs Cleve had finally left. "We've got our marching orders then! I gather you're spending your summer holidays with me. Because I'm your uncle. And I'm helping you to get over being an orphan. And you might be coming to live with me permanently." His eyes roved over Harry's face. "What did you *say* to her? You've got her eating out of your hand. Who taught you how to handle women?"

"I lived with me mam for twelve years… she's just like me mam."

Mr M. threw back his head and laughed. It was the first time Harry had ever heard him laugh. It wasn't to be the last.

The best day was the day they climbed Hedgehope. They went on the bus, a little battered muddy country bus, that groaned and rattled and squeaked its way round the tight bends; with a conductor who seemed to know everybody by name, and asked about all their friends and relations. A conductor who received parcels from people who weren't even travelling on the bus, and gave out the parcels to others who were eagerly waiting at bus-stops. Silly little parcels, like a half-dozen eggs in a bag, or a bundle of rhubarb. And he didn't charge them anything; just doing it out of the goodness of his heart, Mr M. said. And one old man got on with a live hen tucked under his arm, a hen that watched Harry with its sharp yellow eye, and pecked at the old man's serge sleeve with a sharp yellow bill. Another old man had a well-grown lamb that bleated all the way, and left droppings in the aisle. And everybody called to each other down the aisle, like one big happy family.

After that, Hedgehope seemed very silent, with just some invisible birds calling from out of the sunwarmed heather, that Mr M. said were curlews. As they climbed higher and higher, the county of Northumberland spread out wider and wider around them, deep rounded valleys and straggles of tiny grey houses.

Mr M. said Hedgehope was the second highest mountain in Northumberland, and that the highest, over there, was Cheviot itself.

"Why didn't we climb that?" asked Harry.

"No view from the top," said Mr M. "Just a great flat-topped muddy old pudding."

Hedgehope gave views all the way up. When they reached the cairn at the top, Mr M. pointed out Lindisfarne, lying like a crumpled lady's handkerchief on the sea, and the Farnes, and Penshaw monument in County Durham, and the mountains of the Lake District, a misty tinge far to the west.

"It's like you can see the whole world," said Harry.

"Oh, there are far better views from the top of Scafell. You can see the Isle of Man, and the Irish coast. And from Mont Blanc…"

"Have you climbed Mont Blanc?"

"Many years ago. As a young man. I'd like to do it again, before I'm too old. If this war doesn't drag on forever…"

"I'd like to climb Mont Blanc. Is it very difficult? Cold? Does the snow on top lie all the year round?"

"You could manage it. If we got you in training for it."

If we got you in training for it; that meant it might really happen, some day. The world seemed to open out at Harry's feet. Not just the view from Hedgehope, but the view from every mountain in the world. Life seemed suddenly to go on forever and ever, and it was marvellous. Life with Mr M. suddenly joined up with life as it had been before the last bomb. The things in between; the burning bricks of home; Mam, Dad, Dulcie suddenly seemed incredibly *small*. Life would go on now; he knew it. As more than being hungry and soaking wet, as more than fighting angry farmers and the sea. Life relaxed, full of good things, as it used to be. When you could take it as it came...

Except that Mam and Dad and Dulcie wouldn't be there to see it. They must be in some hole in the ground by now. If they'd found anything of them at all.

They were so far away now, so small.

He suddenly found himself just standing crying there.

Mr M. didn't make a fuss, or tell him to cheer up and stop it. Mr M. just gently turned away, to let him cry in private.

Except Mr M.'s shoulders were gently shaking...

Was Mr M. crying too? That made it easier somehow. Nothing to be ashamed of.

When it was all over, Mr M. led the way without a word, down the southern slopes of Hedgehope. There was more grass, between the clumps of heather and bracken, and the air was stiller and warmer, out of the wind. It got quite hot, descending, and there were lots of big fat flies trying to drink your sweat.

So Harry was glad when they came to the craggy hollow, where the little stream they'd been following became a waterfall, into a pool the colour of dark slate, amidst slopes of velvet green grass.

"Cor, I could just do with a swim," said Harry.

"Thought you might." Mr M. reached into his big rucksack with a smile, and produced an old towel, and dark blue bathing trunks. "There's a place to change, behind those rocks."

Harry took the towels and trunks, and went behind the rocks. Somehow, he knew the towel and trunks had been here before; someone else had changed here; someone else had bathed. When Mr M. watched him jumping in and splashing, he would be really seeing someone else. He knew what Mr M. wanted him for; to fill up a boy-sized hole inside himself. That was OK. That Harry felt able to do. It was no more than he'd done for Artie. The only difference was that he'd always known Artie would go away some day, and he had the sudden, breathtaking idea that Mr M. wasn't going away anywhere, ever.

He jumped and splashed a lot, even after he'd had enough. Mr M. must get his money's worth too.

When he finally did come out, shivering and goosefleshed, because the mountain water was pretty cold, Mr M. was busy pumping up an old brass Primus stove, on which a billy-can of water was boiling.

"Tea," said Mr M. "Nothing like a mug of hot tea after a swim. And cake. Plenty of cake."

Afterwards, they sat side by side, watching the fall of the water. A little breeze had got up, that blew the thin stream to one side, so it wavered like smoke, never the same.

"D'you know what shepherds do with orphaned lambs in these hills?" asked Mr M.

"No," said Harry abruptly. He hoped it wasn't something horrible, that would spoil the wonderful day.

"They find a ewe, whose lamb has died. And they take the skin off the dead lamb, and tie it round the living lamb, and put it to the ewe... and the ewe smells the smell of her dead lamb, and takes to the living lamb inside the skin. It works, it really does."

"I'm glad," said Harry.

"It's nature. It sounds brutal, but it works. You get one happy ewe and one happy lamb."

"Yeah," said Harry.

There seemed no need to say more.

Chapter Eighteen

"I wouldn't have liked to live with Saint Cuthbert," said Mr Murgatroyd. "He only changed his boots once a year. The other monks had to drag the old ones off him. And he used to wander about all night praying, so the other monks couldn't get any sleep. They must have been quite glad when he went off to Inner Farne."

"That's not what they taught us at school," said Harry, leaning his elbows on the wall next to Mr M.'s, just touching, in a companionable sort of way. "They only taught us he was holy and converted the heathen."

"Schools!" said Mr M. "I sometimes think all schoolmasters should be stood up against a wall and *shot*. They never teach boys anything interesting, or anything they really want to know."

"Too right," said Harry. That was what the Australian airmen said, who were billeted in Whitley Bay. It sounded slick and tough and grown-up. He watched Don, foraging through the long grass below the outer wall of Lindisfarne Priory. "Don's fine now."

"Paw healed up wonderfully. He's a fine vet, is Mr Harper…"

Harry put his mind out of gear and watched the sunset, as the virtues of Mr Harper were extolled once again. Mr M. couldn't half go on; must be being a schoolmaster. But there were far worse things than going on. At least the awful silences were gone. Silences were comfy now, though rare. And Mr M. could look him in the face at last. Even when he talked about his son; or Harry talked about his mam and dad.

Mr M. said that crying was good for you, even for *men*. But he had never cried again. And neither had Harry. But they'd watched birds, and walked along beaches, and gone sea-fishing, once all night. And come home with a good catch of flatfish, and fried some for breakfast.

And Mrs Cleve was as pleased as Punch with both of them. She said Harry was filling out, and Mr M. looked ten years younger. Mr M. said she was like a hen with two chicks.

"One week of the holidays left," said Mr M. suddenly.

"Yeah," said Harry smugly. "We can go sea-fishing again."

"I don't mean that. I mean I'll have to get back to work, and you'll have to get back to school. What school were you at?"

"The High School," said Harry automatically. But the blue sky seemed to darken, the glitter go off the water between them and the mainland. "I can't go back there…"

"No, no," said Mr M. reassuringly. "But if you went to the High School *there*, you can go to the High School here. The Duke's School, at Alnwick, where I teach."

"Wouldn't mind that, I suppose."

"Very gracious of you. We'll have to get you a uniform; but you'll be entitled to extra clothing-coupons with being bombed out…"

"I got some coupons in my attaché case," said Harry quickly. "Mam was careful. She had a lot left."

"Yes… but," said Mr M. "We can't go on living from hand to mouth, you know. We can't go on pretending you're my nephew forever… people have to be informed. Everything's got to be regular and above board." He suddenly sounded very schoolmasterish. "We must do things properly. We can't go on like this."

"I don't want to go back," said Harry. "Going back will ruin everything. Who *cares*?"

"Your Cousin Elsie…"

Harry shuddered. "She won't want me. She's got six kids of her own and they live in two rooms in Back Brannen Street. It's a *slum*. My mam and dad couldn't stand her. But she'll still make trouble."

But it wasn't just Cousin Elsie. It was *everything*. He'd turned his back on North Shields forever. You didn't climb all the way up a mountain, just to chuck yourself off the top and fall all the way back down again.

"That's enough, Harry!" Mr M. spoke quite sharply. "We are going back to North Shields tomorrow and we're going to set things straight. Then we come back here, and make a fresh start… it won't take more than a few hours, for goodness sake."

God, thought Harry bitterly. Grown-ups. You tell lies for them. You find them flat on the floor and pick them up and make them happy again. And then they start getting bossy.

He had a wild thought about getting his stuff together again, and sneaking off with Don in the middle of the night. But life was no good without your own person, and he'd never find another person as kind as Mr M. And he was tired, tired of the road.

"All right," he said. "But you'll be sorry."

He never spoke a truer word.

Chapter Nineteen

"C'mon," said Mr M. briskly. "We can't hang about all day. I've got the car started. She's going a treat. Don's in the back already. *He* can't wait to get moving."

Harry got up wearily, and said goodbye to the kitchen, with its big hanging oil-lamp and twin rocking-chairs, each side of the fireplace, where they used to sit of an evening. Then he said a long goodbye to Mrs Murgatroyd, who twined about his legs on the doorstep.

"Oh, come *on*," called Mr M. "We'll be back in a few hours." Don barked one enthusiastic bark, from the back seat of the car.

Harry pitied the innocence of dogs. He got in and slammed the car door, like a prisoner slamming the door of his own cell. As they drove out, he said a silent goodbye to the goats, and the chickens and the geese.

"*Lovely* morning for a drive," said Mr M. "Lucky I've got enough petrol. I get it for helping with the evacuees – I shouldn't be using it really. But you're going to be an evacuee soon, I suppose. My evacuee. Really, we've hardly got time to get things sorted out, before school starts. You'll need football kit and…"

He went on and on making plans, as they drove through the bright morning. Harry didn't listen. He was saying goodbye to his kingdom. The kingdom where Mr M. was king and he was prince. It was easy, being a prince with Mr M. You only had to be yourself, and run and laugh and ask questions and help with everything like the goats and hens, and everything was a pleasure. He knew exactly what Mr M. wanted. They'd been lifting potatoes in the garden last night, Mr M. turning over the ground with the spade, and Harry feeling in the loose soil for the exciting small round smooth cool shapes of the new potatoes. Then his hand had closed round something shrivelled and large and soggy and yuk. He'd pulled it out with a squeak of horror and seen it was another potato.

"That's the old man," said Mr M. "That's the potato I planted in the spring, that the plant grew out of. The old man dies, but he gives us all these new potatoes."

And suddenly it was all clear in Harry's mind. The old man potato was the father, and the new potatoes were the sons. The life in the old man was passed on.

"Chuck him back," said Mr M. "His job's done. He's content."

And suddenly Harry realised that Mr M. had been quite content to die in his own good time, when he'd passed on all the things he knew to all the sons he taught. And all the things he owned to his own son.

But the new potato had died before the old man. In the blazing wreck of a battleship off the coast of Malaya. And turned Mr M.'s whole world upside-down.

Until Harry had turned up. The new new potato. He wanted nothing in the whole world except to be Mr M.'s new new potato.

Except Mr M. was ruining *everything*. The kingdom was behind them now, destroyed, gone forever. And now the car, running sweetly along, was rolling up the map of Harry's journey too. Holy Island had vanished behind, where he'd fought the gang and fought the tide and won. They passed the old lady's house, then saw in the distance, near the cliff, the upward-pointing barrels of Artie's anti-aircraft guns. And the pillbox where the RAF man had given him a watch. And even a thin trail of smoke, emerging over the cliff edge, that might have come from Joseph's chimney.

And the chip shop at Newbigin, and the old boat he and Don had hidden under, the endless day after the fight with the farmer. They were coming to the Blyth ferry, and the place where Don had scared off the two men.

It was all undone in less than an hour, all that sweat and pain and hope and despair. All the times he'd won, and all the times he'd lost. He'd done it all for *nothing*. The whole journey, the whole kingdom by the sea, was only a few minutes' drive in a car.

The old familiar scenes began to close in around him, like prison warders. The Haven and the chip shop at Tynemouth. And still Mr M. prattled on about arranging school dinners, and what class he might hope to be in at the Duke's School, and how he'd teach Harry to carve shepherd's crooks in the long winter evenings.

"You'd better direct me from here," said Mr M. "I'm quite lost now."

Oh, Mr M., how right you are, but you don't know it.

"Left," said Harry. "Left again. Right here."

And then they were outside where his house had been.

All there was left was the sagging garden gate, and a few straggly bits of Dad's old privet hedge. Beyond, everything was flat, with weeds starting to grow among the bits of broken brick. It looked like nobody had *ever* lived there. Were bits of Mam and Dad and Dulcie still down there, under the earth? Or had they dug enough out to be buried respectably in Preston Cemetery? He gave a great shudder... even Mr M. noticed. He put his arm round Harry's shoulder.

"Sorry, son. But you had to see it. You had to say goodbye properly. You couldn't go on running away forever. Now it's done, we can go."

"Go?" said Harry. "Go where?"

"The warden's post, I think. They know... what happened to people. They keep records."

"First right, second left," said Harry, staring at the clutch and brake-pedals, with Mr M.'s feet on them. He just felt sick. He just knew what was coming was utterly terrible; it hung over him like a thundercloud.

The wardens were friendly and sympathetic. You could tell the raids had almost stopped for the summer, because the wardens weren't tired to death, or grey with seeing too many horrible things. There was almost a holiday atmosphere in the brick warden's post. Two of them were sitting outside on small wooden chairs, getting a sun tan. The dartboard looked well-used.

The Head Warden got down a great thick grimy book, like the secretary's petty-cash book at school.

"What date was it roughly?" he said gently.

Harry told him. The warden licked the end of his great thick calloused finger and turned the dog-eared pages.

"Baguley," he said. "Baguley. Man, woman and child…" Then he said, "Hallo, that's funny. They're down here as being dead, but then their names have been crossed out again. Hey, Bill, you know anything about this?"

Bill came and looked, but he didn't know anything either.

The third man, Tommy, didn't know any more, except that the crossings-out were official. "Mebbe they were dug out alive after all. By the heavy rescue. The heavy rescue might know. They're in Prudhoe Street…"

Somehow, Harry got back into the car. He knew they hadn't been dug out alive from that heap of blazing rubble he'd left. It was all a balls-up, a cruel crazy balls-up. He didn't even get out of the car when they got to Prudhoe Street. He left it to Mr M.

Mr M. came back after a very long time. He got in and said, in a low voice, "They dug down through your house. They found *nothing*."

"Maybe they were… all burnt up."

"The man assured me they would've found *something*. They always find *something*."

Harry had an awful vision of the chicken that Mam had forgotten about one over-merry New Year's Day, and left far too long in the oven. He nearly threw up there and then.

"They suggest we try the hospital," said Mr M. very low and gentle. "They said they'd know at the hospital. The mortuary's there too."

Mr M. was gone a long time at the hospital. Harry stared at the nurses passing in their starched uniforms. They just didn't seem to *mean* anything. He stroked Don's ears. That helped a bit.

Then Mr M. came back, and his voice was all weird. "They *were* here," he said. "All three of them. William Baguley, Mary Baguley and Dulcie Margaret Baguley in the children's ward. I've seen their records. Those were their names, weren't they?"

"Yes," said Harry, "those were their names."

"They were all quite badly hurt. Your dad had a broken leg, and your mam crushed ribs, and Dulcie had a lot of cuts from glass. They all had a lot of cuts from flying glass. But they've gone. Dulcie was the last. She was discharged a month ago."

"But," said Harry. "But." He didn't believe a word of it. This was all just bits of writing on paper. He'd *seen* the house burning with its evil blue flames.

"Town Hall," said Mr M. briskly. "The Town Hall will know what happened to them. They told me how to get to the Town Hall."

It was as well they had; Harry could never have told him.

At the Town Hall, Mr M. was much quicker. "They've been rehoused. Number eleven, Chestnut Road, the Ridges estate. Do you know it?"

That proved it was all a lie. Mam and Dad would never go and live on the Ridges. The Ridges was where the slummy people lived. Mam and Dad would have *died* before they would go and live at the Ridges. But Mr M. was off again, driving like mad, full of excitement, the excitement of the chase.

Harry stared dully out of the windscreen, as the jungle-like front gardens and broken fences of the Ridges closed in around him. People on the Ridges smashed up their front fences for firewood… it was all a dream, a terrible mistaken nightmare. It must be three other people, pretending to be his family on the Ridges for some criminal reason. Half the people on the Ridges had been in prison for nicking and all that.

"Number eleven," said Mr M. "Come on." He had to nearly drag Harry out of the car. They walked with Don up the cracked ugly front path, past a garden full of weeds. His dad would never have had a garden full of weeds.

Mr M. knocked. There was the sound of footsteps coming.

The front door opened slowly.

Dad was standing there. He was leaning on a stick, and he had terrible scars, on his face and bare arms. He didn't look at all well, and he had on a very baggy and awful pair of old trousers.

But it was Dad. He looked at Mr M. enquiringly then he looked down and saw Harry.

"You little bugger," he said angrily. "Where've you been? You've had us worried out of our minds."

Mam had burst into tears and hugged him; then made a cup of tea in some very crude and ugly cups. Then they all sat round, except Dulcie, who stood by Mam's chair for a cuddle, with her thumb in her mouth, and listened with eyes like saucers.

"We was running down the garden to the shelter," said Dad, "when the bomb hit. It must have blown us clear into next door's garden, and knocked us senseless. First thing I remember was waking up in hospital.

"But Jack Brightman the warden came to see us. They found us in Simpson's garden – number seven – so they just thought we were the Simpsons, and got an ambulance and got us into hospital…"

"What about the Simpsons?" asked Harry.

"They were away on holiday. It was Smith's Dock holiday week."

Now at last Harry remembered. Remembered the warden that terrible night saying that the Simpsons were safe in hospital. Remembered thinking there was something funny about the Simpsons being at home at all. But not being able to work it out...

"And what the hell have you been up to?" asked Dad angrily. "Where the hell have you been?"

"The wardens said you were dead," said Harry. "So I just went away."

"Ran away," said Dad, his voice full of disgust. "A big lad like you, running away?"

"Running away," said Mam. "I've cried myself to sleep every night, worrying what had happened to you."

"Running away!" said Dulcie. "An' you weren't even *scratched*. You were in the *shelter*. Cowardy cowardy custard." She snuggled tighter into Mam's arm, like she owned her. The scars on her face didn't make her look any prettier, and her dress was grubby.

Suddenly, Harry really hated her. Her always running to Mam telling tales, her always sucking up to be Dad's little pet.

"Mam," said Dulcie. "I'm frightened of that big dog. He's staring at me. He wants to bite me." She started to snuffle a bit, like she always had.

"That's *my* dog," yelled Harry. Don was just sitting

peacefully, with his tongue out because he was thirsty.

"*Your* dog?" said Dad in an awful voice. "What makes it *your* dog?"

"I found him. He was the only friend I had."

"Well, you can just bloody well lose him again," shouted Dad. "You're not bringing a great dog like that here. We can hardly feed ourselves, let alone a great humping dog like that."

Harry looked at Don, at that faithful face. That had gone through so much with him. And Don looked back at Harry, as ever, his great brown eyes warm with adoration.

"He'll have to be put to sleep," said Dad, with great finality. "You'll never find the owner now, you bloody little fool. Fancy picking up a great hungry animal like that. Have you got no sense?"

It was too much. On the one side, there was Don, and the open air, and the great winding sunlit coast of Northumberland. His whole kingdom, that he'd found for himself, made for himself. And on the other side, these shabby angry bossy people in their disgusting Ridges house, full of whining self-pity for what *they* had suffered. Narrow, narrow…

He stood up. He said, "If Don goes, I go."

"Go where?" gasped Mam, turning very pale, and

clutching her neck. "What does he mean, Dad, *go*?"

Dad glared at Harry, and Harry glared back at Dad. There was a long, long silence, in which an awful lot was said.

Harry and Dad would never be quite the same ever again.

Oh, some things would get better, no doubt. Dad would get back to work, when his leg was better. Dad was a good worker, and made good money, and they wouldn't stay long on the Ridges. But...

Dad had never seen a gannet dive. He had never seen the dawn come up over the breaking waves of Druridge Bay. He would *never* understand. None of them would ever understand, not even Mam.

Harry had grown, and they hadn't. Harry had grown too big for his family, as if he'd drunk from some magic bottle like Alice in Wonderland. And Dad knew it. And hated it.

It was Mr M. who broke it up. Gently.

"I'd be glad to look after the dog for you," he said. "He'll be company for me."

"Right, that's settled then," said Dad. "I'm beholden to you. And for bringing this young fool home." But he didn't sound beholden; he didn't sound grateful. He sounded pretty angry underneath.

Mr M. knew. Mr M. got up to go. His shoulders dropped a bit, but his face was very kind.

"I'll see you to the car," said Harry, glaring at his family, daring them to try to stop him.

They went out to the car. The car that was still waiting to take them back to the glorious kingdom. Don got cheerfully on to the back seat, but looked puzzled when Harry didn't get in. Mr M. got into the driver's seat, and wound down the window, and sat staring into space.

"I *told* you," said Harry. "I *told* you we shouldn't have come back."

Mr M. looked up at him, amazed.

"I want to stay with you," said Harry. It was the truth.

Mr M.'s face lit up a little, through the bleakness.

"I'll write and let you know how the dog gets on," he said.

"I'll write every week," said Harry. "*Twice* a week."

"Steady on," said Mr M. "Once a month will do. Don't make your father jealous. He's a good man really. He's been through a lot."

"So've you."

"I shall get over it," said Mr M. "Thanks to you. And Don here. We'll look after each other. I think we'll manage."

And Harry thought he might. But he added, "I'll come and see you both. As often as I can. I'll hitch-hike in the holidays. Like the soldiers do, when they go on leave."

"You're welcome. If you can manage it. Go steady though. Don't make trouble for yourself."

"I'm nearly thirteen. I'll soon be able to do what I like."

"None of us can ever do that," said Mr M. warningly. "Not even when we're grown up." Then he said, "Cheerio," with a tremble on his lips, and put the car into gear and drove away.

As they turned out of the road, Harry caught a last glimpse of Don's face, peering at him through the back window.

Then he went back inside. He paused in the hall, hearing Dulcie's voice.

"Who was that man? I didn't like him, and I didn't like that dog."

"Funny sort of feller," said Mam. "He talked very posh. Not *our* sort. Not our sort at all."

"I wonder if he's married," said Dad. "Or if he's one of *that* sort…"

Harry walked in. "He was married," he said. "But his wife died. And his son was killed on board the *Repulse* off Malaya."

That shut them up. But he stared at their faces, and wondered how he was going to keep his own mouth shut, over all the years.

The years before he got back to his kingdom by the sea.

More than a story

Spotlight on Robert Westall

Robert Atkinson Westall was born in North Shields, Northumberland, on October 7ᵗʰ 1929.

He spent his childhood on Tyneside and his wartime memories later inspired many of his novels for children.

Bob 1939, age 10.

"Stanley and I set off on our bikes to look for the War … We worked out ways of fooling German bombers. If they machine-gunned us from the air, we'd pretend to fall down dead, then get up and run again, then pretend to die again. This would ruin their estimate of civilian casualties.

We lived on our bikes, looking for Defences, which seemed in perilously short supply. Every little bit of barbed wire went down in our notebooks, even the thin strands round farmers' fields, which didn't really count but we put them down just the same. Then real Defences appeared: single pom-poms on the Bank Top; armed trawlers. We inspected them daily, looking for improvements, and making sure the crews knew their job."

Excerpt from 'A State of War', a memory from the author's childhood in his own words.

He studied Fine Art at Durham University, before serving two years' National Service in the army. He completed a post-graduate degree in Sculpture at the Slade School of Art in London. He was a teacher for many years, and later a journalist.

Bob with his dog.

Robert, usually known as Bob, first began writing articles for newspapers and periodicals. However, when his son Christopher reached the age of twelve, he felt the need to share what it had been like for him, aged twelve, during the war, so that their experiences would stand side by side.

Westall wrote the memories to read to Chris, then put the notebooks away in a drawer, with no thought of publication. When Lindy McKinnel later read the notebooks, she encouraged him to submit them to a publisher. This eventually became *The Machine Gunners*.

The Machine Gunners tells the story of a group of children living in the North of England during the Second World

War. One boy can't believe his luck when he is scavenging for war souvenirs and finds a fully-operational machine gun in a crashed aeroplane, complete with dead pilot. The consequences of such a find are far-reaching.

Bob's parents (right) and neighbours. His father is wearing his ARP warden's uniform.

The Machine Gunners won the prestigious Carnegie Medal in 1975. It was the first of many accolades. Westall won this award for a second time in 1981 for *The Scarecrows*. In 1989 he won the Smarties Prize for *Blitzcat*, and in 1991 he won the Guardian Award for *The Kingdom by the Sea*.

As well as books set in the war, Westall is equally renowned for his ghostly novels. Cats are also a recurring theme in his work.

In 1983 *The Machine Gunners* was dramatised as a TV serial for the BBC.

Robert Westall died April 15th 1993 aged 63. He wrote about fifty books, some of which were published posthumously.

His partner, Lindy McKinnel set up The Robert Westall Charitable Trust, which contributed to the founding of Seven Stories, the Centre for Children's Books, in Newcastle-upon-Tyne.

Bob and his son, Christopher.

Novels by Robert Westall

The Machine Gunners (1975)

The Wind Eye (1976)

The Watch House (1977)

The Devil on the Road (1978)

Fathom Five (1979)

The Scarecrows (1981)

Futuretrack 5 (1983)

The Cats of Seroster (1984)

Urn Burial (1987)

The Creature in the Dark (1988)

Ghost Abbey (1988)

Blitzcat (1989)

The Promise (1990)

The Kingdom by the Sea (1990)

Stormsearch (1990)

Yaxley's Cat (1991)

The Christmas Cat (1991)

The Christmas Ghost (1992)

Gulf (1992)

Size Twelve (1993)

The Wheatstone Pond (1993)

Falling into Glory (1993)

A Place for Me (1993)

A Time of Fire (1994)

The Night Mare (1995)

Harvest (1996)

The Robert Westall Walk

Robert Westall used his childhood home of Tyneside as the backdrop for many of his books. Much of the countryside that Harry passes through, and the landmarks that he mentions, are real places that Westall drew upon for inspiration.

Modern day Tyneside has changed since the since the war – there is even a road in North Shields called Robert Westall Way! But it is still possible to visit the area and, with a little imagination, summon up sights and sounds of the author's youth. The Robert Westall Walk is a trail which starts at his birthplace at 7 Vicarage Street – marked by a blue plaque – and travels approximately two and a half miles to its finish in Front Street, Tynemouth, through the landmarks of Westall's own boyhood and those of his characters.

The following are some of the landmarks in the area that that feature in *The Kingdom by the Sea*:

St Peter's Church
There are a few remains of this building that was later moved to Balkwell Green. Known locally as the Sailors' Church, this is the church Harry tells the man on Lindisfarne that he attends every Sunday with his mother.

Prior's Haven

The small cove where Harry discovers the abandoned dog Don and then lives under an upturned boat.

Tynemouth Pier

Tynemouth Harbour is protected by two piers. It is under the arches of the North Pier that Harry hides from an air raid.

Marshall's Fish & Chip Shop

Sited in Front Street, this is where Harry buys his tea in his first days on the run.

∿ • You can find out more about the Robert Westall Walk at: www.northtynesidewalks.co.uk

For a slightly different route, you can download an audio tour to follow from: www.westallswar.org/2007/10/robert_westall_trail_audio_gui.html

Lindisfarne

Also known as Holy Island, Lindisfarne is a small island off the coast of Northumberland. A causeway connects the island to the mainland and is flooded by the tide twice a day.

Just like Harry, visitors are able to walk between the mainland and the island, following the marked path. Just like Harry, it is also possible to get caught by the rapidly rising tide, so it's important to check the local timetables before attempting a crossing. And be warned – it's three miles, so it's probably better to go by car!

Although there is a small population on Lindisfarne, it is now largely a nature reserve. It is a haven for birdwatching and many rare breeds have been spotted in its quiet seclusion.

There's also the ruins of a monastery, founded around AD635. Saint Cuthbert, the patron saint of Northumberland, was later an Abbot there, and also became Bishop of Lindisfarne.

The most distinctive landmark on the island is Lindisfarne Castle. Originally a Tudor fort, the ruins were restored by the famous architect Sir Edwin Lutyens in 1903. It stands on a rocky promontory overlooking the coast and is now owned by the National Trust.

You can find out more at:
www.lindisfarne.org.uk

Pillboxes

In *The Kingdom by the Sea*, Harry uses an old deserted pillbox as a temporary hiding place.

What is a pillbox?
A pillbox is a low concrete fort, built on the coastline of Britain, where soldiers would stand watch for enemy planes. They were built in a hurry prior to the invasion of Britain that was expected in 1940. They were positioned at strategic points around Britain, largely on the eastern and southern coasts, but also on some parts of the west coast.

Why are they called pillboxes?
The answer to this question can not be known for sure, but supposedly the name comes from the varying shapes of the forts and the fact that from above they look like the boxes used to store medicinal pills.

How were they used?
Depending on their size, they were intended to hold a garrison of up to ten men, armed with rifles, machine guns or small anti-tank weapons. Some were equipped with mountings for anti-aircraft fire.

How were they disguised from the enemy?

The army had different ways to hide the structures from view. One way was "merging", which means they were built into the ground and hidden by the landscape around them. Another way (as in the case of the one found by Harry) was to disguise the pillbox as another kind of building. This was commonly some kind of house or cottage, but other types were used also such as barns, mills, haystacks and even cafés.

How many pillboxes were there?

During WWII over 18,000 pillboxes were built. It's estimated that less than 7000 are still standing today.

Key Events in World War Two

1939

31st August: Evacuation plans announced in Britain in preparation for the outbreak of war.

1st September: Hitler invades Poland.

3rd September: Britain declares war on Germany.

1940

7th January: Rationing of basic food items starts in Britain.

10th May: Winston Churchill becomes Prime Minister.

14th May: The Home Guard is formed.

26th May – 4th June: Evacuation of Dunkirk.

10th July – 31st October: The Battle of Britain. This was an aerial battle, the first major campaign to be fought entirely by the air forces.

23rd August: First all-night bombing raid on London, marking the start of the Blitz. Over next few months important industrial and military centres around the country were targeted, including Coventry, Bristol, Southampton, Plymouth, Liverpool, Birmingham, Manchester and Tyneside.

1941

1st **June:** Rationing of clothes and furniture begins.

7th **December:** Bombing of Pearl Harbour in Hawaii by Japanese planes.

8th **December:** United States of America enters the war.

1942

January: The first American troops arrive in Britain.

23rd **April:** The Luftwaffe start bombing Exeter, Bath and other historic cities in Britain. These became known as the Baedeker raids because they were targeting cultural centres.

1943

18th **January:** The Luftwaffe resumes bombing London.

1944

6th **June:** D-Day, the Normandy Landings. The first operation in the Allied invasion of Europe.

13th **June:** First V1 Flying bomb lands on Britain.

8th **September:** First V2 Rocket lands on Britain.

1945

8th **May:** Victory in Europe (VE) Day. War in Europe ends.

15th **August:** Victory in Japan (VJ) Day. War against Japan ends.

Want to Know More?

- Find out more about what life was like for children in WWII:
  www.bbc.co.uk/history/ww2children/

- WWII timeline:
  www.worldwar-2.net/

- Imperial War Museum:
  www.iwm.org.uk

- Beamish Museum online. An archive of life in the north east, including an extensive range of recorded recollections of wartime experiences:
  www.beamishcollections.com

- Pillboxes – photographs and information by region:
  www.pillboxes.co.uk

Seven Stories

"Some people say there are only seven stories in the world, but a thousand different ways of telling them. Seven Stories is about the thousand ways."

Seven Stories, the Centre for Children's Books, is based in Newcastle-upon-Tyne. It was opened in 2005, and was founded as a place to celebrate British children's writers and illustrators. To date it still provides the only exhibition space in the UK wholly dedicated to children's literature and displays original manuscripts and artwork from some of the nation's best-loved books.

The Robert Westall Charitable Trust played a significant role in the establishment of Seven Stories and one of the galleries is named in the author's honour. Westall's archive is on permanent loan to the Centre and in 2006 housed a fascinating, interactive exhibition of his work: *Westall's Kingdom – A Writer's Life*.

The display included manuscripts and artwork from *The Kingdom by the Sea*, and a reconstruction of the secret den from *The Machine Gunners*, complete with machine gun, comics and other artefacts from the period.

The Centre has plenty to enjoy for visitors of all ages and a rolling programme of events throughout the year. From dressing up and drama, storytelling sessions, to creative writing, illustration and crafts. Plus there are regular events given by contemporary authors and illustrators. And there's also a brilliant bookshop where you can top up your collection of books by your favourite authors.

If you want to visit Seven Stories or learn more about their current exhibitions, you can find out how at www.sevenstories.org.uk.

Want to Read More?

Non-fiction

The Making of Me: Robert Westall, A Writer's Childhood
Scenes from the author's childhood, in his own words.

Children of the Blitz by Robert Westall
A selection of letters and wartime memories sent to the author after the publication of *The Machine Gunners*.

Fiction

When Hitler Stole Pink Rabbit by Judith Kerr
Anna's family is forced to flee Germany in 1933 after her father has published anti-Nazi articles.

The Amazing Story of Adolphus Tips by Michael Morpurgo
Lily's adored cat goes missing when the US army requisitions her village for army manouevres in preparation for D-Day.

Billy the Kid by Michael Morpurgo
Billy might be 80 years old, but inside he's still the eager youth who was lucky and talented enough to play football for Chelsea. Then war broke out and changed the course of his life forever.

Hitler's Daughter by Jackie French
When Mark hears the story of Hitler's daughter it haunts him. Could it have been true? Did Hitler's daughter really exist? If Mark had a father like Hitler, could he love him?

A Tale of Time City by Diana Wynne Jones
When Vivian is evacuated from war-threatened London in 1939, she expects to be staying in the countryside. Instead, she is whisked away to Time City, where rogue time-travellers are plotting to take control. If they succeed, Time City and History as will be destroyed.